PROLOGUE

I check out Mr. Ward's classroom early, find dark walls covered with poetry hanging in picture frames bright as jelly beans.

Who wrote all these poems? And where exactly does Open Mike Friday take place?

My eyes travel the room until I notice a low stage, off to the side. It's not very big, but there's a spotlight hanging overhead, and in the center of the stage is a microphone just begging for somebody to grab it. Me? I'm a newspaperman. What am I even doing here?

I look back over the last week, trace the thinking that brought me to this class.

Like every other day, a week ago started off with breakfast.

BETWEEN THE LINES

ALSO BY **NIKKI GRIMES**

Jazmin's Notebook

Bronx Masquerade

The Road to Paris

Make Way for Dyamonde Daniel

Rich: A Dyamonde Daniel Book

Almost Zero: A Dyamonde Daniel Book

Halfway to Perfect: A Dyamonde Daniel Book

BETWEEN THE LINES

NIKKI GRIMES

PENGUIN BOOKS

PENGUIN BOOKS
An imprint of Penguin Random House LLC, New York

First published in the United States of America by Nancy Paulsen Books,
an imprint of Penguin Random House LLC, 2018
Published by Penguin Books, an imprint of Penguin Random House LLC, 2019

Visit us online at penguinrandomhouse.com

THE LIBRARY OF CONGRESS HAS CATALOGED THE NANCY PAULSEN BOOKS EDITION AS FOLLOWS:
Names: Grimes, Nikki, author.
Title: Between the lines / Nikki Grimes.
Description: New York, NY : Nancy Paulsen Books, [2018]
Summary: A group of high school students grow in understanding of each other's challenges and forge unexpected connections as they prepare for a boys vs. girls poetry slam. Includes author's note about foster home care.
Identifiers: LCCN 2017025067 | ISBN 9780399246883 (alk. paper)
Subjects: | CYAC: Poetry—Fiction. | Authorship—Fiction. | Interpersonal relations—Fiction. | High schools—Fiction. | Schools—Fiction. | Family life—Fiction. | Poetry slams—Fiction.
Classification: LCC PZ7.G88429 Bet 2018 | DDC [Fic]—dc23
LC record available at https://lccn.loc.gov/2017025067

Printed in the United States of America

Penguin Books ISBN 9780525515159

1 3 5 7 9 10 8 6 4 2

Design by Marikka Tamura.
Text set in Baskerville Com.

For Jacob Bruch, who never gave up waiting for a sequel,
and for Kendall Buchanan, my brother.

DARRIAN LOPEZ

BREAKFAST ON THE BOUNCE FOR FATHER AND SON

¡Perfecto! If I was writing a story about this morning, that would be my headline. I drop two waffles into the toaster, smiling to myself. Papi looks up from *El Diario*, wondering why. I shake my head, sorry he's reading the wrong paper. For me, it's the *New York Times.* The old man is cool otherwise, though, driving a city bus double shifts sometimes just so he can keep replacing the clothes I grow out of. He doesn't say much, but he loves me enough for two.

I wash one waffle down with milk, grab the other for the road, and head out of the door.

"Later, Papi."

On the way to school, I run into Zeke and Shorty, guys from my neighborhood. As usual, they're talking smack.

"You watch, Shorty," spouts Zeke. "I'm gonna be the biggest thing in hip-hop since Heavy D."

"What you been smokin'?" counters Shorty. "You can't even sing! But me? I got serious moves on the court, plan on bein' the next Kobe Bryant. Look out!"

They laugh to take the edge off of dreaming bigger than they believe. I keep my dreams to myself. I don't need their laughter. Besides, I have to pay attention to these cracked sidewalks so I don't trip or step on broken whiskey bottles or the dirty syringes that turn up everywhere.

"So, what you plan on doing to get your Black ass outta the Bronx?" Zeke asks me.

"You mean my Puerto Rican ass." I've told Zeke a million times, I'm not Black.

"Quit lying! You Black. You just got an accent," he says every time. And every time, I shake my head.

For the record, my mother's not Black. My father's not Black. I'm. Not. Black. We are *puertorriqueño. Boricuas.* From the island. But what the hell. Black and Brown people all get treated the same, anyway.

I look at Zeke and shrug, then jog ahead, disappearing around the corner.

BROWN BOY BETRAYS RACE

That's what they'd say if they knew I planned on writing for the *New York Times.* Let's face it, some of those papers got a bad habit of getting Black and Brown stories wrong. We all know it. But I figure the only way to get our stories straight is by writing them ourselves. So I'll get in there, show them how it's done.

Yeah. Only, I'm not sure how exactly to get started.

I whip out my notebook, flip past the last local news story I wrote, and scribble: *See Mr. Winston for help.*

Writing my plans down makes them feel solid. I smile all the rest of the way to school.

• • •

Lunch bell rings just in time. Stomach's growling loud enough to wake the dead. I jump up, head for the door. The *Times* lying unfolded on the teacher's desk stops me cold.

"Mr. Klein?" I ask. "Can I borrow your paper over lunch? I promise not to get mustard on it."

"No problem," he says. "I'm done with it, anyway."

I scoop up the paper and tuck it under my arm.

TEACHER'S CASUAL KINDNESS REMEMBERED

The *Times* is like my bible: If it says something, it must be true. You can't say that about too many papers these days. Seems like half of what gets printed is based on outright lies. I'm all about truth, though, so I figure the *Times* and me are a good fit.

I hit my locker, grab my sandwich, and sprint to the yard so I can read without interruption. I find a quiet spot, unwrap my sandwich, unfold my paper, and gobble up both before the bell rings.

Home. Ready to chow down on anything I can find. I dump cap, jacket, backpack in a sloppy trail on my way to the kitchen and plant my face in a bowl of cold cereal. I don't even hear Papi coming in early.

"Darrian!" he barks. "What's your stuff doing all over the floor? You know better."

"Thorry," I manage, mouth full of flakes. Papi must

not be too mad. He goes quiet in there. But just in case, I swallow fast and pop into the living room to clear my mess.

Papi's in the middle of the floor, flipping through my news stories. He looks up when he hears me.

"*¿Qué es esto?*" he asks, waving the notebook at me. "Some new kind of homework?"

My ledger of headlines and neighborhood features is hard to explain.

"Not homework," I whisper. "Just . . . stories I write . . . for practice."

"*¿Por qué?*"

I clear my throat, ball my fists, ready for the laughter I'm afraid of.

"Practice for being a reporter at the *New York Times*."

I grit my teeth, wait for it. Papi grunts, hands me the evidence of my crime.

"Go on, *hijo*. Pick your stuff up. Put it away."

That's it. That's all he says.

I breathe, forgetting all about being hungry.

Later, I flop on my bed, bury my head under a pillow.

Now I've gone and done it, said out loud what I want to do, to be. But how do I get there from here? Where do I start?

First thing in the morning, my questions carry me to the library to see Mr. Winston. Before I reach his desk, I notice a girl hunched over a table I can barely see the top of, there are so many books spilling across it. I can only make out one title without stopping to stare like some creep. It says *e. e. cummings*, all in small letters. Is that supposed to be a name? 'Cause that's weird. I mean, who writes their name in all small letters? Never mind. I'm here to see Mr. Winston. He's the only person I know who loves newspapers as much as I do.

"So, you want to be a newspaperman," says Mr. Winston.

"Yes, sir."

"Well, here's what you do."

I whip out my pen to take notes.

"Get excellent grades so you can attend a good journalism school. Apply for a summer job at a local paper so you can see the work up close. As for right now, keep studying the dailies. And learn as much as you can about all sorts of writing, not just articles but essays, short stories, even poetry."

I quit writing when he gets to that last thing.

LIBRARIAN LOSES HIS MIND

"Poetry? Why do I need to learn about poetry?"

"Because poetry, more than anything else, will teach you about the power of words. If you're going to be a reporter, that's something you need to understand."

I nod, only half convinced. Poetry. That's a new one.

I drag myself in the door that night, a Brown balloon with all the air let out.

How am I supposed to learn about poetry?

I'm folded up in a kitchen chair, head on the table, when Papi comes in.

Thwap!

Something lands heavy beside my head. I crack one eye open, see the bold black ink of a familiar logo that gets my attention. I sit up straight, rub my eyes.

"Folks leave newspapers on the bus almost every day," says Papi. "I usually toss these out at the end of my shift, along with *El Diario* and all the other papers. *Pero* now that I know you like these ones so much, I figured I'd bring 'em home."

Two days' worth of *New York Times* are right there, rolled up next to me. My eyes turn from the headlines to my dad's face, then back to the paper.

"*Gracias*, Papi," is as much as I can manage between all that grinning and feeling like something's stuck in my throat.

GIFT LEAVES BOY SPEECHLESS

Man!

Next day at school, I hear some kids talking about Open Mike poetry readings that happen in Mr. Ward's class on Fridays. He taught tenth grade last year, but he moved over to eleventh grade this year, which works out for me since that's the grade I'm in. We're only one week into school, so I beg my guidance counselor to switch me over into his class. I beg with puppy eyes so she won't have a chance to say no. She shakes her head, tries to hide a smile, and signs me up.

Now I'm here, checking out Mr. Ward's classroom before the rest of the class piles in.

I notice one of the poems, shaped like a Z. That gets me to look closer. The shape doesn't make sense until I read it. It's a pretty cool poem about Zorro and how most people think of Latinos as one stereotype or another, because all they know about us is some fairy tale they've seen in the movies or on TV.

"Raul Ramirez wrote that one," says a voice behind me. I practically pee in my pants! I didn't hear anybody come into the room.

"I'm Mr. Ward," he says. "And you are?"

"Darrian Lopez," I manage, still breathing heavy. "I just signed up for your class."

Mr. Ward smiles.

"So, what do you think of the poem?"

"It's pretty good. I mean, I like it," I say, trying not to sound too impressed.

"Well, these are all poems by last year's class. I took them all down at the end of the year and turned them into an anthology. I made photocopies of my favorite poems, though, so that I could hang them back on the wall. By the end of this year, there will be new poems. Maybe one of them will be yours."

"I don't know about that," I say. Anyway, that's the end of our conversation, because the class is filling up. I wait until everyone sits down so that I can tell which seats are still free.

Mr. Ward welcomes me into class quietly, which I'm happy about. He motions me to the back, where there are a couple of empty seats. I take one near a pretty Black girl with straight blond hair. I don't know how I'm going to feel about poetry, but I know I like the scenery!

I pay attention when the roll is called.

"Valentina Alvarez."

"Here."

I wonder about the personalities behind each name.

"Angela Marie Bailey."

"Here."

"Li Cheng."

"Here."

I turn my head. Wait! That's the girl I saw in the library! Cool. Now I'll get to ask her about that e. e. cummings book.

"Marcel Dixon."

"Here."

"Freddie Houston."

"Here."

"Darrian Lopez."

Oh! That's me. "Here."

Every now and then, my mind wanders. I don't catch every name.

"Kyle–"

"Here."

I notice there are more girls than guys.

I like that.

"Jenesis Whyte."

"Here."

Jenesis, huh? So that's who I'm sitting next to! Her name makes me think of beginnings. A new class. A new year. This is going to be interesting.

"Yesterday," says Mr. Ward, "we started talking about narrative poetry. A narrative poem, simply put, is a poem that tells a story. In order to write a narrative poem, then, you must first decide on–what?"

"Your story," says Jenesis.

"Exactly. Open your notebooks and, for the next few minutes, I want you to think about a small story, or an anecdote from your childhood, and write about it in a paragraph or two. Keep it simple."

"What kind of story?"

I'm glad someone else asks so I don't have to.

"You decide. It could be a favorite memory of someone in your family, a road trip or vacation that stands out, something that happened in school when you were little. You are the narrator. You choose the story. But keep in mind, you will be turning this into a poem, so keep the story short."

Story. I can do that.

"Close your eyes," suggests Mr. Ward. "It may help you to focus."

Mr. Ward is right. I close my eyes and concentrate on Papi, on how we used to be together when I was little. As soon as I do, I remember the rattle of newspaper as Papi folded *El Diario* on Sunday morning at the breakfast table. I remember scrambling up onto his lap so I could see what he was looking at. Thinking of those days makes me smile. I open my eyes and start to write.

That night, our assignment is to turn our paragraphs into a poem. Closing my eyes doesn't help much now. All I know about poetry is it rhymes, so I keep trying to find words that rhyme with *newspaper*. Forget it!

> *In the mornings*
> *on Sundays*
> *Papi and me*
> *we always*
> *sat at the breakfast table*
> *with* El Diario
> *before I was able*
> *to read or understand*
> *the newspaper*
> *in Papi's hand . . .*

I know. Pretty lame.

The next time we have class, Mr. Ward starts off by asking, "How many of you wrote your poem?"

Almost all our hands go up.

"And how many of you tried to write your poems in rhyme?"

My hand slips up, along with maybe half the kids.

"And how did that work for you?"

The last question was followed by a lot of grumbling, including from me.

"I'm not surprised," says Mr. Ward. "Most people mistakenly think that all poetry has to rhyme. In fact, they use the words *poem* and *rhyme* interchangeably. But rhyme is only one element of some forms of poetry, and there are many forms that don't employ rhyme at all."

Damn! Now you tell me!

TEACHER BURIES THE LEAD

"Instead of trying to force your words to rhyme, I want you to start thinking of poetry in a different way. A poem paints a picture using words. So a narrative poem is a poem that tells a story and paints a picture using words. You want to use language that is lyrical, that is descriptive. If rhyme comes to you naturally, it's fine to use it. But if it doesn't, that's fine, too. *Rhyme* and *poetry* are not synonymous! Okay?"

I copy down everything Mr. Ward says, word for word. After school, I pull out my paragraphs about Papi and me reading the newspaper, and I start working on a brand-new poem. This time, I give up worrying about rhyme and start paying more attention to lining up words with the same letters and turning words into pictures.

I won't lie. It takes a lot of practice. Like, instead of just writing *paper* when I'm talking about the special paper the daily news is printed on, I try to find words that tell you how that paper feels when you touch it. Writing this way takes more time, but it's worth it. The poems I end up with are pretty decent. They still have a little rhyme in them, though. Even so, I can't wait to show the latest poem to Mr. Ward.

The following day, Mr. Ward introduces some kid named Tyrone from his class last year. He invited him to drop in to kick things off for our first Open Mike Friday poetry reading. I thought I knew what to expect. Not even close.

TYRONE BITTINGS

"Y'all got no idea, but you're in for something deep. Trust me," I tell Mr. Ward's class.

"Mr. Ward asked me to help y'all get this year's Open Mike Friday started. I'm totally pumped to do it, especially since I can't hang so much this year. I've got some schedule conflicts since I've decided to go for a JC—that's *junior college*, for those of you who don't know the lingo. I need to kick up my grades in math, in science, in history, in . . . well, in pretty much every subject but English. Time to man up if I'm gonna chase my dreams, as my homey Wesley 'Bad Boy' Boone would say. Anyway, I'll be dropping in during my study period, when I can. I'm not in class officially, but I'm gonna be like—Teach, what do you call it in college when you sit in a class, but don't get credit?"

"Audit," says Mr. Ward. "But you can't actually audit a class in high school, Tyrone."

"No? Well, it sounds cool. Anyway, Mr. Ward gave me a special pass so I can drop in whenever I don't actually need study hall to study. Guess I'll be doing my homework at home!"

That got me a laugh.

"So listen, y'all heard a little bit about Open Mike

already, right? Well, last year, we had it for the first time. It all started when Teach did this lesson about the Harlem Renaissance. To me and my homey Wesley, the lesson was all blah, blah, blah until Teach started reading poetry. Sorry, Teach, but it's true.

"Teach read this one poem that made me think of rap, which I know something about, seeing as how I gots mad rhyming skills myself and know how to tell a story with a beat, you feel me? So I asked Mr. Ward if I could read one of my raps. A couple other kids had poems they wanted to read, too. So Mr. Ward started this regular Open Mike poetry reading in class, and next thing we know, kids from all over the school are practically busting down the door to get in on the action."

"A slight exaggeration," says Mr. Ward.

"Well, okay. But a lot of kids were getting passes to come to our room whenever we were doing Open Mike, and that ain't no lie.

"What I loved best about it was getting to know everybody. I mean, before Open Mike, we were all in our own separate little groups, thinking we were so different from each other. But when people started sharing who they were through their poetry, turned out we were more alike then we were different. Black, White, Puerto Rican–it didn't matter. Truth is truth, and everybody bleeds red.

"The kids in that class? They are all my peeps now. And they helped me believe in myself, in my dreams of what I could be. Bet you didn't know poetry could do all that, huh?

"Y'all should look around the room, check out the people you're sitting next to. You might think you know who some of them are, what they're about. You've got no clue. By the end of a semester doing Open Mike, you will.

"Cool? Okay. Let's get this thing started! Who wants to go first? I'd read one of my poems, but I don't want to show you up."

Everybody laughs, which is exactly what I wanted.

"No, I'm just kidding. I'll get the ball rolling. After that, the mike's all yours.

"Oh! And one more thing: At the end of the semester, there's gonna be a poetry slam, Team Boyz against Team Girlz, so get ready for a little competition. And you know the Boyz are gonna crush it. It's throwdown time, people!"

Truth

by Tyrone Bittings

Yo, yo
I know
you think a poem
ain't nothing but
a reason for a song.
I hear you, but you're wrong.
Trust me:
A poem can split skin
and let the blood run red.
A poem can turn the clock back,
help you crack the code of you.
A poem can strip away fear,
leave a messed-up mind clear
to understand what's going on
deep inside the heart,
the one part
of our world
where we can maybe make some sense,
since, suddenly, unnatural disasters
crash the nightly news
on instant replay.
High crime and Homeland Insecurity
are the order of the day.
But, hey,
rap and rhyme is one way
to strap on your own power,

at least for an hour.
So slide a pen in your holster,
lock and load whatever
words you choose.
Use them to cry, to shout,
to whisper–whichever.
Just step up, step up to the mike
and let your truth fly, loud,
proud, raw.

DARRIAN

Turns out my hand has a mind of its own. For some reason, it slips up right after Mr. Ward says, "Who's next?" Now my knees are noisy as maracas. *¡Dios!*

Tyrone flashes me a look like *What are you waiting for?* I shake off my nerves and make it to the mike before my legs give out.

Act like you're reading a news story, I tell myself. *You've done that a thousand times. Just not for an audience. Is it hot in here?*

Okay. Here goes.

LOPEZ LEAPS OFF POETRY CLIFF

Headlines

by Darrian Lopez

On Sunday mornings,
I used to curl up
on the cushion
of my papi's lap
while he read
the newspaper to me
like a bedtime story.
I understood little,
except the familiar
hum of his voice,
the silk of the paper,
thin as tissue,
the kiss of ink,
its temporary tattoo
remaining on my fingertips
after I helped Papi flip
through sports
and local news.
Sometimes, my love
for newspapers
and for Papi
feel like
the same thing.
They say newspapers
are dying out,
but I'm not about

to give up
my sweet addiction.
Besides, searching
the headlines of the day,
hidden in the folds
of a newspaper,
is one of the few things
Papi and me
still have in common.

As I read my poem, I see a few kids nodding their heads like they know what I'm talking about. But does that mean the poem is good? Just okay? Or are they being, you know—polite?

As soon as class lets out, I run up to Tyrone.

"Hey!" I say.

"Oh! Hey, man," says Tyrone. "Wazzup?"

"Well, I was wondering if you have time to maybe look at my poem. Maybe tell me how I can make it better, since you're so good. I'm new at this poetry stuff."

"Sounds like you're doing pretty good to me," says Tyrone. "Although, you could throw in a few internal rhymes. Like—let me see the poem."

I hand it over, watch Tyrone scan the lines.

"Okay," says Tyrone. "Here's what I mean . . ."

On Sunday mornings,
I used to curl up
on the cushion

of my papi's lap,
happy to listen
to him read the daily
newspaper to me
like some G-rated
bedtime story.

"You get what I'm saying? A little internal rhyme, here and there, will help punch up your piece. But hey, man. I gotta run."

"Yeah! Sure! Thanks, man," I say. "I'll try that. Then maybe I could–"

Tyrone takes off down the hall, leaving my last words in the wind.

"–catch you later."

The following Monday, Mr. Ward talks to us about some poets from the Harlem Renaissance. Most of us know what that is, of course, but we don't know anything about someone named Jean Toomer, or this book called *Cane*. Except for Li. She seems to know all about him. Or *her*? Jean could be a man or a woman, right? Anyway, Mr. Ward calls on Li.

"Do you have a favorite poem by Jean Toomer, Li?" asks Mr. Ward. Li looks around, then clears her throat.

"Yes, I do," she says, sitting up even straighter than she was before.

"Could you read it for us?"

Li slowly stands, turns to a page in her notebook, and

reads–no, recites–the poem. She's hardly looking at the page, so I figure she's got it memorized.

"Thunder blossoms gorgeously above our heads / Great, hollow, bell-like flowers . . ."

Li takes her time so each word hangs there a second before she goes on to the next one. When she's done, nobody moves. Nobody.

"That was beautiful," says Mr. Ward. "Now, can you explain what it means?"

Li twists her ponytail. "I'm not sure," she says. "It's . . . complicated." She goes on in a rush, "But I love his choice of words, how they pop on the tongue like cherry tomatoes when you bite into them, the way they send a burst of flavor all over your mouth. I love that." Li sounds out of breath.

"Why, Li," says Mr. Ward, "you sound exactly like a poet."

Li blushes, but she doesn't deny it. She just lowers her eyes, sits back down, and smiles. I smile, too, but my eyes are wide open, and they're on her.

LI CHENG

I love my first name. Depending on how you spell it, it can either be Chinese (Li) or American (Lee). Or both. Like me.

I'm all Chinese and all American. That's a lot of contradictions to squeeze into one small body.

My facial features scream Chinese, but my lips can't even manage an entire sentence of Mandarin because my parents did not encourage it. We celebrate Chinese New Year as well as American holidays like Thanksgiving. However, while my mom serves turkey, most of us prefer the *huo guo* (hot pot) she makes to go with it.

My closest girlfriends are Asian, and of course at school we all eat lunch together. In some ways, we're very much alike, except that most of them were raised to be quiet and soft-spoken, while I was taught to speak my mind with confidence, like my brother, even when I'm speaking to my parents. And I do. Except when it comes to poetry. Why do I hide my love of poetry? That's a long story.

My father started off life as the poorest of the poor, in a tiny village in China, living off rice and sweet potatoes because it was all his father could afford. For his family, meat was a luxury they could only dream of. At seven, he sold sea cucumbers in the market and gave the money to his mother to help feed his brothers and sisters. Then, when he was ten, he escaped to Taiwan by boat, hoping to find better opportunities. Eventually, he emigrated from Taiwan and came to America. He landed in New York City with only a few dollars in his pocket. His story sounds like the lyrics for a song, but it's one nobody would want to sing.

He searched for work in Chinatown and eventually found two jobs: one cutting strawberries for an ice cream maker, and the second washing dishes at a restaurant. He used the money to pay for college, where he met my mother.

Today, they enjoy life in "the golden land," still working hard so their children can go to the best schools and find secure company jobs with good benefits and pensions. An uncertain life in the world of literature is not part of my parents' master plan for me.

Sometimes, I'm dying to ask my father, "BaBa, why did you struggle so hard to give me a life with choices if you won't let me make my own?" But I'm a respectful Chinese daughter. I know when to speak my mind and when not to, so I lower my eyes, say nothing, and hide my dreams in the silence. For now.

Maybe I'm not as different from my friends as I thought.

I keep my poetry to myself and work on it in my room. Sometimes my mother barges in to see what I'm doing. She looks over my shoulder, sees my poetry journal, and grunts.

"What is that?" As if she doesn't know.

"It's poetry, MaMa."

A second grunt.

"Useless," she says. "Is your homework done?"

"Yes."

"Carry on, then."

I'm excited about the new school year. My Vietnamese friend, Mai, told me about an English class where they hold Open Mike poetry readings. Mai's family moved to California over the summer, so she won't be attending, but she thought I might like it. I pretended to be only mildly interested, but inside, I was jumping up and down.

One week in, and I already know this year is going to be the best, thanks to Mr. Ward and Open Mike Fridays.

I'll just have to keep my eyes off Darrian. There is no way he would ever notice a plain girl like me.

Threads

by Li Cheng

How can I explain
the duality of Li?
The muffled sounds
of mah-jongg tiles touching,
clicking together,
flips a switch in me
as my parents follow
the ritual
of the ancient game.
The Mandarin calligraphy
clinging to our walls
sends my soul sailing
to rice paddies
oceans away,
to the land of silk,
red sunrises,
and the jade mountain peaks
my parents
often speak of.
China whispers
through their blood,
You are part mine.
Remember!
And I nod, silent
and ashamed

that my untrained
American lips
are unfamiliar
with my ancestors'
local lingo.

DARRIAN

There's something about this *chica*. I don't know, but I can't stop staring at her. She's not even my type. She hardly has any curves, at least none that I can see. But how can you see anything under those big, baggy shirts she wears? Why does she dress like a boy?

Her skin is perfect, though. My fingers are itching to touch her face. She's not pretty exactly, but something about her is . . . beautiful. Maybe it's just the poetry. I don't know. She's got my heart thumping, though. I'll have to keep an eye on her.

CHINESE CHARMER CASTS HER SPELL

JENESIS WHYTE

The first week in a new school is the worst. The staring and the stupid questions are annoying. Questions like, "What are you, exactly?" And "You know you got blue eyes, right?" No, moron, I've never looked in a mirror! How do people come up with this stuff? You think I had a choice when God was handing out the eyes? Like I could've said, "Hey, God, you gave me blue eyes by mistake. I'm supposed to have brown eyes because I'm Black." Yeah, right. That's the way it works.

I don't know why my hair is blond. I don't know why my eyes are blue. I wish I did.

My social worker says I was just two years old when my mom brought me to the hospital with a fever. She turned me over to the doctor, and said she was just going to fill out the papers at the nurses' station. Only she never made it there. She'd told the doctor her name was Wilhelmina Whyte, and after she disappeared, the police tried to find anybody with that name. But maybe she just made it up. Whatever her name was, she was gone.

They say she was pretty young, probably a teen mom with no clue how to raise a baby. That's what I'm thinking. That's what I want to think, 'cause I could maybe forgive her for that. Anyway, apparently she never mentioned my father, so there was no chance he was going to show up at the hospital to claim me.

My social worker said after a few days, the hospital turned me over to social services. That's when I began to experience the joys of foster care. Yeah.

The first homes were fine, as far as I remember. I had my own bed, regular meals, and a few toys of my own. In one home, there was a dog who felt like my own because he always liked to sleep at the foot of my bed. He was a German shepherd puppy named Lucky. Maybe I liked him because he was small, like me.

Yeah. There were a few nice homes, but I never got to stay in them for more than a year or two. Sometimes it was because the family was moving out of the county. Sometimes they started having children of their own and couldn't handle any extras. Sometimes I didn't get along with their children–whatever. There's always a reason. All I know is that a phone call will come one day, and the next I'll be packing my plastic bag for the move to the next house of strangers.

In the beginning, my social worker thought I'd be one of the lucky children who get adopted. Hah! White families weren't in the market for a kid with brown skin, and Black families weren't too crazy about having a brown baby with blond hair and blue eyes. Both said I'd never fit in with the rest of their family. Not much I could do about that, now, was there? I swear, if I couldn't disappear inside of books, I'd have lost my mind by now. Narnia was enough to do it, back when I was a kid. I'd climb inside that wardrobe every night, and I'd take off running. Later, I just wanted books about girls, the stronger the better. Their stories reminded me that I was one of them, that I'd make it in whatever foster home I was sent to.

As I grew older, it was harder to find homes at all. People didn't want a kid who was old enough to talk back, never mind one who'd be quick to report them if they decided to smack her around. And nobody seemed to want a kid who was–what was the word they used? Sullen! Yeah. That was it. Tell me, what kid wouldn't be sullen after years of being dragged from one foster home to another?

Anyway, I survived. That's something, right? Now here I am in home Lucky Number Thirteen, wondering how long this one will last. I hope I can make this work for four more semesters. Eleventh grade, twelfth grade, and then I graduate. A month later, I'll turn eighteen, and I'm out after that, anyway.

The hardest thing about my life? Knowing almost nothing about the people I come from. Not knowing if I ever will.

I walk down the street or wander the aisles of the supermarket sometimes, staring at strangers, hoping to catch a glimpse of somebody with my eyes, my nose, the shape of my mouth, even. There's got to be someone in the world I look like, right? Someone I take after.

Or maybe that kid Tyrone was right when he tried to hit on me, saying I was the first of my kind, like Eve back in the Garden. Yeah. Right!

Quit it, Jenesis! This thinking gets you nowhere fast. Homework. What did I do with my homework assignment? Oh, here it is.

Mr. Ward says we should try to write a poem, see where it takes us. Says we should look inside, find what is true, and tell it in a poem, maybe read it for Open Mike. Is he crazy? I'll write something to read for class, but he can forget all about that "truth" stuff. For now, I'll give them a made-up story so maybe they'll leave me alone and go study somebody else who doesn't fit their mold.

Blue Eyes Squared

by Jenesis Whyte

I see you staring at me.
You be boring a hole in my soul
as if the alchemy
of your curiosity
could somehow turn
these blue eyes brown,
but you might as well forget it.
You frown at my blond curls,
even though girls with hair
the color of sun
the color of spun gold
are supposed to have more fun.
At least, that's the story
they try to sell me on TV.
Yeah, I'm different, but
don't call me freak
or assume I'm the only one.
There are bound to be
other brown beauties
with pale blue eyes
eerily like mine,
wearing smiles crooked
in exactly the same way,
noses that scream
matched set.
Are there more like me?

Yeah, you bet.
When I find them,
I'll fit in without question,
never mind that
the world thinks
I'm odd as H-E–
well, you get it.

DARRIAN

I'm not buying that there are people wandering around who look just like Jenesis.

Big as this city is, I've never even seen one other Black person with blue eyes, let alone natural blond hair.

BLACK GIRL TELLS TALL TALE

Seriously! I'm not going to be the one to call her on it. But once I get to know Jenesis, I'll definitely be asking her what that's all about, and why she's not happy being special.

MARCEL DIXON

My middle name is Dunbar. Marcel Dunbar Dixon. I know. It's a lot of name to walk around with. I work out every day just to stay strong enough to carry the weight.

Marcel was my grandma's idea. She got it from some old French guy named Marcel Marceau. You could probably look him up online, since he used to be famous. He did this thing called "mime." He could, like, use his body to create the illusion of something that wasn't even there. I'm telling you, he could pretend he was in a box and then fight his way to get out, and you'd totally believe it. Or he'd act like he was in a tug-of-war with somebody, and you'd see him pull an imaginary rope. And his face would be all scrunched up like he was straining hard, tugging on that rope, hand over hand. Then, the invisible person on the other end would jerk the line, and Marcel would get dragged a few feet in that direction, and you could see the strain in his muscles and everything. It was wild. And it would go on like that, back and forth, back and forth, until Marcel finally let the rope go. It was imaginary and it was real all at the same time.

Grandma said Marcel had some kind of magic in him, 'cause he could make you see things that weren't even there. She figured I could use a little magic. Turns out I wasn't the one who needed it. She should've given that name to my dad. Maybe if he'd had a little magic, he could've skipped being dragged off to prison.

My middle name, Dunbar, was strictly from my mom. She used to be a big reader—at least that's what she tells me. I don't see her reading much these days. Not like she's got time between her two jobs. But she used to have time. Before. And she read a lot of stuff, novels mostly, but poetry, too, especially from the Harlem Renaissance. Now, most people pick Langston Hughes as their favorite poet from back then, or maybe Countee Cullen. Not Moms. Her favorite was Paul Laurence Dunbar.

Moms won't admit it, but I'm pretty sure she was banking on me being a writer when she picked Dunbar for my middle name. She keeps saying she wants me to be whatever I want to in life, but I saw her face the first time I gave her a poem for her birthday. She read the poem out loud, just before she cut her birthday cake, and I swear her eyes burned brighter than all those lit candles combined.

I keep Dunbar to myself, like most folks do with their middle names. He's the poet in me, the man with the rhymes. And rhyme is my sanity, my secret weapon. Or it was, until Moms ratted me out to the principal.

I got in a fight last week. No big deal, but I wouldn't talk about it. The principal asked me what happened and I wouldn't say. Meanwhile, the butt-head I laid into said I started it. Which wasn't true, but why should I say anything? What was the point? It was gonna be my fault no matter what, right? 'Cause I was the "troubled kid." Yeah. Folks love their labels. So I just sat there in her office all afternoon, saying a whole lot of nothing. At the end of the day, she just shook her head and sent me home.

That night, she called the house, and I heard her and Moms jabberin' about second chances, and how important it is for me to learn to express myself, to channel my anger, blah, blah, blah. And next thing I knew, Moms was telling her, "Well, I know he writes poetry sometimes."

That was last week.

Now I'm in Mr. Ward's class. The principal hopes it'll do me some good, keep me from slipping through the cracks. Whatever.

I'll sit here, but I'm still not talkin', not till I'm good and ready.

For now, any poetry I write is strictly for me.

Troubled

by Marcel Dixon

What is it
with people and their labels,
as if the way they mark me
makes them able
to understand who I am
or why?
"Troubled kid"
tells you exactly nothing
about the trouble
my pops has seen
or Moms
or me.
We stare from windows
caged in iron,
in state prisons
or rented rooms,
which are only better
by degree.
We are forced
to survive outside
the neatly mowed landscapes
of your imagination.
Our stop on the train station
is worlds away
from your manicured lawns

and lives
and the lies you tell
about the days
of racial discrimination
being in the past.
Quit asking
why I'm angry
or I'll tell you.
Then, you'll have to
change your ways,
only you don't want to
'cause this system
works for you just fine
the way it is.
But since you asked,
here's one thing
that makes me mad:
Poverty,
and a mother too busy
to keep an eye on her kids
'cause she's working
two jobs
to keep us fed.
That's reason enough,
ain't it?
There are more, of course,
but don't force me
to spell it out now,

'cause I'm a troubled kid
and I am not
in the mood.

DARRIAN

This brother is nobody to mess with. I saw him light into a kid last week, and I wouldn't want six feet of muscle coming down on top of me like that. Good thing the principal was able to break it up.

Marcel may not be fighting now, but I don't think it would take much. He's hanging off his seat like he's about to take off any minute, or wants to. Every now and then, he balls his fist like he's practicing for a dustup. Like he's ready to jump in the ring and take his bad day out on anyone stupid enough to get in there with him.

RAGE ON PARADE

Seriously. Mr. Ward is the coolest teacher I know, but Marcel is staring him down so hard, flashing him so much anger, I'm surprised Mr. Ward hasn't gone up in flames.

What is his story?

They say his dad was in prison. Is he thinking about heading in the same direction or what? Do I even want to know?

LI

Darrian. I like the name because it's different. It's a mystery. It doesn't tell you what he is, or who. I've heard him speak Spanish, but there's nothing Spanish about his first name.

Darrian and Li. I write the names together in my mind, but not on paper. The thought of anyone seeing it makes my cheeks burn.

"Li! Did you hear me?" My friend Jingyi snaps me back to attention. Her name might mean "quiet," but she is actually quite loud!

I look around the lunch table and find three pairs of eyes staring back at me. Maylin, Hanna, and Jingyi, whom we all call Jing. We've known each other since first grade.

I pick up my chopsticks, bend over my lunch, and pick up a sticky rice roll. I chew slowly while the girls talk about boys and college. Boys mostly.

Suddenly, a silence falls over the table and I look up to find out why. Darrian slips into the empty seat next to me, and I almost choke.

"Hello!" says Darrian.

I fight to keep my chopsticks from shaking.

"Hello."

"Sorry to interrupt," he says to everyone, then turns to me. "I just wanted to tell you how much I liked your poem the other day."

"Oh." He's probably just saying that to be kind.

"'China whispers through their blood,'" he quotes. "I love that line."

So, he did pay attention!

"Thank you!" I say, my cheeks starting to get warm.

"There was one thing I didn't understand, though. I was born here, but both my parents speak to me in Spanish, and they expect me to speak Spanish, too. So why didn't you learn Chinese?"

He really did pay attention to my poem! "Mandarin," I say, correcting him. "My parents did not encourage it. They wanted my brother and me to be American in every way, and to them, that meant speaking only English."

It feels funny talking to a stranger about all of this. Why did he come over here, anyway?

"Oh. That makes sense," says Darrian. "Anyway, I just wanted to tell you how much I liked your poem, and I'm looking forward to the next time you share on Open Mike Friday. See you in class," he says, then slips away as quietly as he arrived.

I suddenly realize that the whole table has been silent all this time.

"Who was that?"

"He's kind of cute!"

"And new! Where did your new boyfriend come from?"

"Would your parents mind that you're dating a boy who's not Chinese?"

"You guys! One question at a time!" I say. "First, I'm not seeing him."

"Uh-huh," says Hanna.

"Second, he's not my boyfriend."

"Sure," says Maylin.

"Third, if he was, my parents wouldn't mind. My brother has already brought home girls who weren't Chinese, so it's no big deal."

"If you say so," adds Jing.

I don't need a mirror to know that my cheeks are red as pomegranates.

I bend over what's left of my meal to hide my face. I'm a little embarrassed, but mostly excited because the impossible happened: Darrian noticed my poem. Maybe, just maybe, next time he'll notice *me*.

Journey

by Li Cheng

We throw words on the wind–
poems, stories.
We hope they rise
like bubbles,
then hitch a ride
on a cool cloud
or cold current
and return to earth as
nourishing raindrops
or fragile snowflakes.
But where will they fall?
Atop Mount Fuji?
Over the Brooklyn Bridge?
And who, if anyone,
will catch them?
It's a kind of miracle
when they land
on the palm of someone
familiar.

DARRIAN

Li closes her eyes when she performs her poems. I like that. It makes me want to crawl into her poems, see what she sees behind her eyes. I get what she's talking about here. Connection. It's what we all want, right? No matter what language we speak.

Entiendo, Li, I whisper.

I hear you.

VALENTINA ALVAREZ

"'Val.' What is that?" my father asks me for the hundredth time. "I named you Valentina. It's a good, strong name, *mija.* Why won't you use it?"

My father doesn't understand. Val is more American. That's what we are, and I want to fit in like someone named Valentina never would. Like my father never will. He still calls himself Ignacio. Does that sound American to you? It's an old argument, only I don't argue anymore. I just tell my friends to call me Val. That's it.

Don't get me wrong. My father is as proud to be an American as I am. Sometimes I wonder how he can be, though, the way so many people put down immigrants. I hate the way a lot of them look down on him sometimes, talking to him in slow, clipped sentences as if he's stupid just because his English is a little rough. They can only speak one language, while my father speaks two, so who's the one that's lacking? Dad forbids me to call such people stupid, but if the shoe fits . . .

When you're an immigrant, you work at whatever job you can get. Dad mops floors and cleans toilets at Stitt Junior High School. But back home, he was *un profesor.*

So was my mother. Some of their friends who emigrated at the same time were doctors, psychologists, librarians, interior decorators, business owners. Now, like my dad, most of them are custodians, street sweepers, or, if they're lucky, driving gypsy cabs in neighborhoods where everybody speaks Spanish.

Immigrants don't have a lot of choices. You don't know the language, and all your credentials come from somewhere else. None of this makes you stupid, though, unless you want to say that a person was stupid for coming to America to begin with. But try telling that to folks who look down their noses at every immigrant they see, or think they see. Most of them can't tell the difference between an immigrant and a native Latino anyway. Your skin is olive and your hair is black? You're an immigrant, as far as they're concerned. Now, that's stupid!

Sometimes I wish our family was as fair as most people from Argentina. It would have been easier to fit in if we were fair. But it's not as if you get to pick the color of your skin. Besides, being fair doesn't help you much if your English isn't good.

Last night, I told Papa for at least the millionth time he should take some courses, work on his English so he can get a better job, but he said he's too old.

"But, Papa," I said, "when people see you cleaning floors, they think you're not smart, and you're the smartest man I know!"

"Don't bother about what people say, *mija*," he told me. "Let them talk. They only prove their ignorance."

I know my father's right. I also know that words have teeth. Sometimes I get tired of the bite marks.

"Papa, cleaning toilets—you are so much better than that."

This made him angry. "Nobody is too good to clean toilets, *mija*! It is honest work! I'm glad to have it."

"But, Papa—"

"Enough! I know who I am. That's what's important—not proving something to some strangers I don't even care about, *¿entiende? I* know who I am. Now, what I want for you, Valentina, is that you go to school, work hard, and decide who *you* are, who you want to be—for yourself. Not for anyone else, *mija*. Not for anyone else."

I knew enough to drop the subject after that, for now, anyway. I gave my father a hug so he would know I love him, even though we don't agree. He hugged me back and sent me to my room to do my homework.

I mentioned that we were studying poetry in school, and my parents gave me some of their old poetry collections to read. I began devouring my father's favorite, a volume by Pablo Neruda. I read for an hour, then began playing with a poem of my own. When I was finished, I signed it *Val Alvarez*.

What You Don't Know

by Val Alvarez

Mi padre, *Ignacio,*
is a book you haven't read.
It's filled with poetry
that can curl its fingers
around your corazón
and squeeze out joy.
Pero *you've never*
cracked the cover.
You scribble crítica
that questions
the measure of the man,
but you've never
peeled back the pages
of his biografía.
You toss el libro
onto the trash heap
marked "Immigrant"
y ustedes dicen *it has no value.*
But, of course,
you are categorically incorrecto,
which you would know
if only you could read
las palabras.
If only you, too,
were blessed
to be bilingual.

DARRIAN

That's right! You tell them, *chica*! It takes heart to live out loud in two languages, to come from another country and figure out how to stand strong on ground your feet ain't even familiar with.

Like Papi had to do.

Like Mami had to do.

I know one thing: nobody in this family is scared of work.

Mami nearly killed herself busing tables at a diner for the breakfast rush, then spending every afternoon cleaning hotel rooms downtown, on her feet all day long. Man. I don't know how she did it. Then breast cancer had to show up and make her life even harder. Mami fought, though. She didn't win, but she sure went kicking and screaming all the way. Didn't you, Mami?

Yeah. She was tough, an immigrant just like Valentina's dad.

I bet she would have liked Valentina.

Me? I like her already. And not just because of her dreamy eyes and those dimples you could dive in. There's a lot more to this *chica* than pretty.

ALVAREZ BRINGS THE HEAT

KYLE NEWTON

Just call me Kyle. Forget the last name. In middle school, kids called me Newt. From there, it rapidly devolved (yes, I have a heightened vocabulary) to Eye of Newt, and by noon of the second day, my fate was sealed. I was the butt of jokes for the remainder of the school year. I'm not interested in that kind of abuse again, which is why, during roll call, the split second I hear the teacher say "Kyle," I shout out "Here!" before he can make his way to the last name. So, for the record, it's Kyle. Just Kyle.

This morning, I left home on the fly, late as usual. Skateboarded six blocks, smooth and easy, without catching one curb or cracked sidewalk. *Whoosh!* I went manual a couple of times, balancing on the back of the board while the front wheels were off the ground, but nothing too fancy. I'm still just an am, after all. (That means "amateur," for those who don't know the lingo.) Anyway, there's no point in trying tricks on the street. There's not enough room. It's hard to carve or make superfast turns when you've got pedestrians every few feet. Like this cute girl who had the nerve to cross my path, her sweet hips demanding my eyes follow them a little too long. I stopped just in time to keep from bailing or smashing into a light pole. Glad my mother didn't see that. She'd have a cow.

You'd think I was made of glass, the way my parents fuss over me. And my poor brother feels practically invisible. He gets fed up with all the attention I get. I can't blame him. So I have a heart condition. Big deal! Unless you see my scars, you'd never know. And it's not like I go around shirtless every chance I get—not that I'd have a problem with it, mind you. I've got great pecs, and my scars make me look kind of tough. Manly. Still, I don't go around showing them off.

My heart condition is just something I have. Some people have asthma; I have a man-made heart valve. I see the doctor for regular checkups, take blood thinners every day, and that's it. I haven't had a major surgery in years.

Okay, so there are certain things I can't do. You know those commercials about joining the military so that you can be all you can be? Well, not me. I can't. Never gonna happen, no matter how many times I dream it. Organized sports? Nope. But the thing is, I'm not sure I'd have been interested in playing them, anyway.

Skateboarding, that's different. The first time I saw someone step onto that little board and sail down the street, I knew it was for me. The Doc said no, of course. Mom said, "Definitely not!"

I took months of saved-up allowance and bought a skateboard three days later.

My heart may be weak, but my head is hard as stone.

When the grown-ups saw I was going to skateboard anyway, they relented. Barely. Mom still looks at my skateboard as if it's a tiny coffin with my name stamped on the rim.

I've got to figure out how to get my folks to let me breathe, especially Mom.

Before You Ask

by Kyle

In, and out.
In, and out.
The breath's a silent gift
we unwrap
moment to moment
from the second we're born.
How many breaths does it take
to scramble up an oak,
or go for a touchdown,
or peel around
a sharp curve
on a sweet board?
In, and out.
In, and out.
I never count breaths
or store them
in a bank for
unimagined tomorrows.
Born with a weak heart,
I'm smart enough to know
any tick, any tock
could be my last,
or yours. So
I just fill my lungs,
dive deep into today,
and–go!

DARRIAN

¡Qué corazón! That scrawny little kid is ten kinds of tough. I don't think I could risk my life like that every day. I've seen this kid slicing up the sidewalk on his way to school. He don't play! Who knew he was sporting a weak ticker? You couldn't tell. Papi would say that boy's got a lot of heart. It's not even a joke.

BOY TAKES HEART ON A WILD RIDE

This guy, I want to know better.

I look around for Kyle at lunchtime, find his table, and slide in next to him.

"Hey, Darrian," says Kyle.

"Hey. That poem of yours was tight!" I tell him.

"Thanks!"

"So, it made me wonder," I say, real easy. "What exactly is wrong with your heart? I mean, it's not like anyone can tell you're sick by looking at you."

"I'm not sick," he says. "Not anymore. Look, when I was a kid, I had to have surgery, and they put a man-made valve in me 'cause the one I was born with wasn't working right. That's it. Simple."

"Wow."

"Yeah. Anyway, I take meds, go see my doctor for checkups, and that's it."

"Damn, man! You say that like it's no big deal," I say.

Kyle shrugs. "Well, I figure I got two choices. I can walk around like I'm half dead, or I can act like I'm completely alive—which I am."

"Yeah," I say. "But if you're not careful—"

"I can die?" Kyle finishes my sentence. "Guess what," he says. "We all could. And we all will, sooner or later. Might as well have some fun while we're here."

I nod, then turn my attention to the slice of pepperoni pizza on my plate.

Kyle takes a couple of bites out of his turkey burger. "*Mm, mm, mm,*" he hums between bites, enjoying that burger like it's his last.

It's cool the way he makes the most of every single moment, every single thing. We should all try that.

"So, Kyle," I say, "you think you're doing the slam?"

"I get it," he says. "You need a token White guy on your team, right?"

Oh, man. I'm all ready to apologize when he cracks a smile.

"Just kidding! I wish you could've seen your face!"

STUDENT HUMOR FALLS FLAT

"You got me," I tell him.

"Sure, I'll do the slam," he says. "It'll be fun."

MARCEL

That White boy's got a pair, I'll give him that. But he ain't got to go through life with a target on his back. For that, his skin would have to be a whole lot darker. Still, I give him props for living life on his own terms. Me, I'm still trying to figure out what those terms are.

The day is over before I know it, and I head home. There's no place for me in the living room when I get there. I'd go to my room if I had one. But I sleep on the couch. The extra bedroom is for the girls. My sisters have taken over the couch and the TV is blaring at them. Mikayla is trying to get the little ones to sit still, but she's not having much luck.

"Hey, Mik."

"Hey."

I land in the kitchen, spread my books over the table. That's where Pops finds me. He walks straight to the fridge, grabs a beer like he does every night. He never used to swig beer. Not before.

One day, after he got out of jail, Pops brought home a job application to fill out. He couldn't get his old job back at the MTA 'cause they don't hire former felons.

I remember watching Pops smooth that application

and start filling it out, line by line. Everything was fine until he got to the question *Have you ever been arrested?* His jaw got tight, and he balled up that paper, threw it across the room, and slammed out the door. It scared me a little, so I went after him. When I got to the corner, I saw him slip into a bar across the avenue. When he didn't come back out right away, I figured he was gonna be in there for a while. He's been throwing back beers every day since.

He buses tables now at a local restaurant. The owner hired him because his son was in the system once. He gets it.

Pops hates the job. Mom tried asking him about it.

"What the hell you want me to say?" he snapped. "Grown man, busin' tables. It ain't right."

Mom never asked him about that job again.

I miss Pops. My old Pops, the one who'd play pickup games with me after work. The one who'd smile. That guy is gone. All his dreams are gone, too. He used to imagine the house he'd buy for us in Queens once he saved up enough from working for the MTA. He left that plan locked up in his jail cell.

"Marcel!" Mikayla calls me. "Come watch Mia and Mariah. I got to get in there and make dinner."

I don't much feel like babysitting, but I don't feel like cooking, either.

"Coming."

Spaghetti and meatballs are on the table by the time

Moms comes in for a quick bite between Job #1 and Job #2. We're all tired of spaghetti, but we can't get food stamps anymore, so we take what food we can get.

I used to hate food stamps.

Ain't life a bitch.

Say Cheese

by Marcel Dixon

"Say cheese"
is something you don't hear
around my house
'cause nobody's getting ready
to smile.
It's been a while since
I saw Dad's mouth
curl up at the corners,
and my mother's pretty much
out of practice, too.
You gotta understand,
the system broke my daddy's heart
when it taught him
justice is just for people
without dark skin.
Too much melanin
can be deadly as cancer,
if you know what I mean.
This harsh reality
makes me wonder whether
the future is something
I should plan for at all,
seeing as how
chances are small
any dreams I might conjure
will survive.

ANGELA MARIE BAILEY

I'm afraid. That's all you need to know about me. I'm afraid. Of everything, and I don't know why. I'm afraid to ask. I'm afraid to wear a new style before somebody else does first. I'm afraid to meet new people. I'm afraid of not meeting new people. I'm afraid of looking like a dork. I am a dork, but I'm afraid of people finding that out. I'm afraid to wear heels because I might tip over and break my neck. I'm afraid if I don't wear heels, no cute boy will look at me. When a cute boy does look at me, I'm afraid to look back. Mostly, I'm afraid of always being afraid. That's why my guidance counselor, Mrs. Wexler, sent me to Mr. Ward's class and signed me up for the poetry slam. (Why on earth did I ever mention to her that I wrote poetry? Stupid, stupid, stupid!) As soon as I realized I was going to have to read my poems out loud, I begged her to switch me to another class. Did she? Of course not! She said I needed to at least give this class a try. Perfect.

Mrs. Wexler thinks if I get up and read my poetry in front of a classroom of strangers, it will help me to be less afraid of things. Did I tell you that Mrs. Wexler is insane? If I get up in front of class and read my poetry, I'll die.

She'll be sorry then! Of course, it won't matter, because I'll already be dead.

"You're up, Angela," says Mr. Ward. "Mrs. Wexler mentioned that you had a poem you'd like to read today, yes?"

That's it, I think. *When this class is over, I'm going straight to that woman's office and give her a piece of my mind!*

Oh, who am I kidding? I'm too afraid to even raise my voice to her!

"Angela?"

Oh, God! I feel sick. I am *sick. If I don't get to the bathroom fast–*

"I'm sorry, Mr. Ward! I have to–"

I feel that first heave and take off running. I make it to the girls' room just in time to puke my guts out.

Ugh! The smell!

Once I'm sure there's nothing left inside my stomach, I go to the sink and spend a good five minutes washing my mouth out. I check my clothes to make sure there's no vomit on them, then slowly start back to class. I might as well. I'd try hiding, but with flaming-red hair halfway down my back, I'd be spotted in no time. I keep thinking about dyeing it, but I'm afraid I'd only mess it up and turn it green by mistake.

"Are you all right?" Mr. Ward asks as I slip back into the classroom. I nod my head up and down, too embarrassed to speak. I go to my seat, but not fast enough.

"Class," says Mr. Ward, "excuse us for a moment. We'll be right back."

Mr. Ward steers me toward the hall and closes the door behind us. I lean against the wall, staring at my shoes, expecting him to ream me out for leaving the room without a hall pass. I'm wrong.

"It looks like you have a bad case of stage fright," says Mr. Ward. "It's okay, Angela. Lots of people have it."

"Sure," I tell him. *No they don't.*

"You don't believe me. Listen, when I was in high school, I took a theater class. I loved acting and I was pretty good at it. But the very first time I had to go onstage, I threw up. Three times!"

"You did not!"

"Yes, I did," says Mr. Ward. "It was so embarrassing."

"Well? What did you do? After, I mean."

"I went onstage and I played my role. Once I got through the first few lines, I was fine. I just had to get started. I think that's all you need, too. If you get those first lines of your poem out, I bet you'll be fine."

"I don't know," I say. "I don't think I can do it, not with all those eyes staring at me."

Mr. Ward is quiet for a moment.

"How about this: What if we turn out the lights? I'll leave one on so that you can see your poem to read it, but turn off all the others. That way, you won't be able to see anyone staring back at you."

"Could–could we really do that?"

"Why not? Come on," says Mr. Ward. "Let's give it a shot."

So now I'm standing in front of the mike, waiting for the lights to go down. The sound of my knees knocking is splitting my eardrums.

Oh, God! I hope my stupid hands stop shaking. If they don't, I won't be able to read this stupid poem on this stupid piece of paper.

Unafraid

by Angela Marie Bailey

My mixed-breed feline
is–

Uhm, is, uh . . .

Is what? I can't read my own stupid handwriting. Jeez! What *is* that? Oh! *Fierce!* That's it. Okay. Breathe. Breathe. It's just you in the dark. Okay? Just start again.

My mixed-breed feline
is a fierce warrior,
routinely stalking dogs
three or four times her size
without a hint
of trepidation.
The neighborhood mice
don't stand a chance.
I've seen her leap
from a windowsill,
skip two stories,
then land on a branch
of a nearby tree
and look back at me
as if to say,
Aren't you coming?
Every day,

I study that
green-eyed sphinx,
trying to discover
the key to her courage,
all the while wondering
how many of her nine lives
she has left.

DARRIAN

I'll bet she's glad that's over! She looked like she was going to faint. That would make for a good headline.

PANICKED POET PASSES OUT

I shouldn't laugh, though. She really looked scared. I think cats are lame, but her poem was pretty decent. A few of us clapped to let her know, so maybe next time she won't be shaking so bad. She gripped that paper so hard, I was sure it was going to rip in half.

Just goes to show you can't judge anybody by appearances. You look at a person and you think their life is perfect. No reason, except they live on a street with no broken bottles, they got clear skin, and their hair and eyes are the colors TV tells you are the best. So that must mean life is a breeze for them, right? That's what I thought about Angela. Wrong.

Mira, you can never go by the surface of things, not if you're a newsman. You have to slip below the surface to find out what's really going on, to find the truth. And the truth is never simple. Nothing is ever what it seems, I'm learning that much.

I see Kyle go up to Angela and whisper something in her ear, then walk away.

"What'd he say?" I ask her, like it's my business.

"He said nobody knows how many lives they have left, so you just have to live. I wish I could do that." Then she walked away, her head down, avoiding eye contact.

Pobrecita.

LI

I arrive at class early, as I always do, leaving extra time to organize my books and pens neatly on my desk. I open my notebook to a clean, crisp page so that I'm ready whenever Mr. Ward starts to speak. His chair is still empty, so I look around the room. There are more girls than boys, which makes me feel a little less isolated, since I'm the only Asian.

Val's hair falls in soft waves today, and her turquoise sweater practically screams *Look at me.* And of course, all the boys do. No surprise. But Freddie also looks nice. Marcel can't stop staring at her. Jenesis is pretty, too, with those blue eyes and her dark skin. And even shy Angela, every red hair on her head perfectly in place, how could you not notice her? I feel like I'm the only plain one.

I look down at my oversize gray sweatshirt and I hear my mother's voice.

"Pretty doesn't matter. Just because you're a girl doesn't mean you can't be smart, confident. Study hard and you can be as accomplished as any boy. In another two years, you can join your brother at Princeton if you want to. Or go to Yale. Or Harvard. Forget about boys and pretty clothes. Concentrate on your studies and you can accomplish anything, just like your brother. There'll be plenty of time for boys and pretty clothes later."

The speech is an old one. My mother has been giving it for as long as I can remember. Hearing the same speech over and over again gives me a headache, but I get it. My grandmother gave my uncle special treatment because he was a boy. Mom spent her life working hard to prove to Waipo that she was just as good as a son. Grandmother never changed, but Mom made sure she and my father treated my brother and I the same. We were equally encouraged to do sports if we wanted to, and to study science and math—whether we wanted to or not.

Sometimes I feel pushed a little, but it's all right. I understand that my mother wants me to be secure in my own abilities. But I look around at these girls, and they seem smart *and* pretty. So why can't I be both? Of course, I'll never be pretty like they are. My eyes are too small, my black hair is too straight and boring, and my skin is too pale. Still, I could put on a little blush, maybe. And some lip gloss. I tug the hem of my sweatshirt, wondering how I'd look in a nice blouse. Then I feel a pair of eyes on me and look up. It's Darrian!

I lower my eyes quickly, and my hair falls over my face. I shove my hand in my jeans pocket and rummage for a rubber band. I ran out of the house so quickly this morning, my hair was too wet to pull back into my usual ponytail. I'd forgotten all about it. Until now.

Big mistake!

I fumble with the rubber band until my ponytail is in

place, then look straight ahead. I pretend not to notice Darrian's eyes still on my face.

"Good morning!" says Mr. Ward, striding into the room. Finally! Now I can concentrate on learning. That's what I'm here for, right?

Sons and Daughters

by Li Cheng

Waipo,
my mother's mother,
adheres to the old tradition
of treating sons like gods
while daughters' egos
are left to wear thin
as rice paper.
Uncle calls me
"the lucky one."
My mother twisted her resentment
into a new rule
for my father to follow,
an understanding underlined
in their wedding vows:
treat sons and daughters
the same.
Fierce as a general,
MaMa holds him to it.
Instead of caring for me
like a fragile flower
so I would bloom,
or station me permanently
near the cooking pot,
they sharpen my mind
like a sword
so I, too, can cut the air

with a thought
or expound on
the periodic table
at a moment's notice,
like my brother.
I'll surely design the next skyscraper,
or pilot a space shuttle,
or accomplish some new,
extraordinary feat
previously unknown
to womankind.
But who will teach me
what to do with
this heavy hair,
this slim girl's body
that will never
grow hair on its chest?
Mother tries her best,
but I am left feeling
half boy, half girl.
Unfinished.

DARRIAN

She doesn't see herself, the beauty of her soul, how it comes out in her poetry. Li. Even the name sings.

I wish there was some way to let her know her mother gave her everything she needs.

At lunch, I see her head for the table she sits at every day with her Chinese friends. But this time, Valentina and Angela wave her over to join them.

Qué bueno.

Everybody can use new friends. Plus, Li is one of us now.

POETRY GANG GATHERS

JENESIS

I'm back at what passes for home these days, not that anyone notices. I stopped at the library for a couple of hours, so Mrs. Knox is already in the kitchen, working on dinner, by the time I arrive.

I slip into my closet-of-a-room, drop my backpack on the small desk, and toss my jacket on the twin bed that's jammed against the wall.

There's no dresser in the room, just some open shelves over the desk where they said I could keep my clothes and books and stuff, including my ratty underwear, which means I've got zero privacy. You know, in case I was planning on hiding drugs or something. Everybody knows all foster kids do drugs, right? I could just stuff them in a pillow if I wanted to, or in my shoes, or underneath the mattress, or in the plastic garbage bag the last home gave me to carry my stuff in. Did they think about that? Whatever.

Mr. and Mrs. Knox have two kids of their own, two girls. Karen, the older one, is mean as hell. Only one of us is a natural blond, and it's not her. She hates that, which is stupid. I can't help the way I look. Why hate somebody for that?

She made sure I knew she didn't like me, right off the

bat. She introduced herself my first morning there by disparaging my clothes. I was on my way to school that first day, and she stopped me in the hall, saying, "I hope you're not going out wearing that crap." I took care of the problem. When she wasn't looking, I went to her room, borrowed a pretty purple shirt without asking, and walked right up to her in the lunchroom later that day.

"What do you think about my new shirt?" I asked, turning this way and that to model for her. Poor girl just about choked on her lasagna.

Naturally, she goes running to her mommy that night, crying about how I stole her shirt. I get yelled at and told to wash the stupid thing and give it back.

"Let her have it," said Karen, pouting. "It's got her stink all over it now."

Fine by me. There's nothing wrong with my stink, and I kind of liked that shirt, so I was happy to keep it.

I got sent to my room without dinner. Plus, no TV. Big deal. I tell you what, though. That little twit hasn't said a thing about my crappy clothes since.

Mr. and Mrs. Knox are all right, I guess. They don't beat me or anything. And I like the way Mr. Knox is gentle with his daughters. If I knew who my father was, that's how I'd want him to be with me. Karen's too mean to know how lucky she is.

Karen and her sister, Cassandra, share a large bedroom down the hall. They've both got dressers. Seems nobody's worried about them having a place to hide drugs. Never mind.

The hours I spent in the library today were all about reading for fun. I've still got my homework to do, so I empty my backpack and get busy.

I've been bent over the desk for more than an hour when my stomach starts to growl. Lunch was forever ago. Naturally, when I walk in the kitchen, I see the family is halfway through the meal. They forgot to call me. Again.

Mr. Knox grunts when he sees me at the door. Mrs. Knox looks up, nods toward an empty chair. There's no place set for me, so I hit the cabinet, snatch a plate, fork, and knife before I sit down. A quick scan of the table tells me just how late I am. The bowl of mashed potatoes only has a spoonful left. There's some broccoli spears (yuck) and one anemic-looking chicken wing. Mrs. Knox follows my gaze.

"There are cold cuts in the fridge," she says, "if you need some more food. You can make yourself a sandwich."

I nod, keeping my eyes on the table. Hide my anger. I'm not much interested in making a sandwich, so I just pick at whatever food is left, starting with the mashed potatoes.

"So," she says to one of her kids, "how was school?" Mr. and Mrs. Knox turn their full attention to Karen and Cassandra. I call them daughter number one and daughter number two. I concentrate on a broccoli spear. Might as well. Nobody asks me how my day was.

That Kyle kid complains about being smothered by his parents, says they care a little too much. Hah! He should trade places with me for a minute, try living with people who don't care at all, see what that feels like.

My stomach growls, still half empty, so I jump up and slap together a sandwich, after all.

"Jenesis," says Mrs. Knox. "Don't forget to do the dishes when you're done."

"It's not my turn," I say. "It's Karen's."

"Is that right?" asks Mrs. Knox. On cue, Karen starts to moan.

"Mom, I don't feel so good. My stomach is bothering me."

"Poor baby! Then go lie down, sugar. Jenesis can get the dishes this time."

This time! This time? Hell! Try all the time!

Karen, who is anything but sick, staggers to her room, stopping just long enough to turn and stick her tongue out at me when her mother isn't looking.

I grind my teeth, ball a fist under the table. What can I do? This isn't the first time I've been told to pick up after some foster parent's lazy brat. If I don't go along with it, they could kick me out. Then what? It's not like I've got somewhere better to go, and they know it. Treat me like a slave. But it's no big deal, long as I got somewhere to live. At least until I turn eighteen. That's what I keep telling myself. That's what keeps me from spitting fire, from tossing bricks.

I finish my sandwich, take my plate to the sink, and run the water till it's hot. I stack the dishes in the tub, squeeze in dishwashing liquid and get busy. Halfway through, Little Miss Suddenly Sick sticks her head in the door.

"Don't forget the pots," she says. I cut my eyes at her,

pull a glass from the dishwater, and let it drop to the floor. Meanwhile, I'm looking straight at her.

"Oops!" I say.

Little Miss Suddenly Sick starts yelling. "Mom! Mommy! Come see what Jenesis just did!"

Yeah, I know. This probably means my social worker is gonna get a call in the morning, but I don't care. I wasn't supposed to be washing these damn dishes in the first place.

Foster Kid

by Jenesis Whyte

I seethe beneath
a mask of I-don't-give-a-damn,
waiting for anger
to burn my bones to ash.
I dare you to
ask me why
there's fire in my eye.
You know what? Never mind.
I'll just tell you.
The answer is SHE,
the twisted, devil-spawn darling
of my foster parents.
There's more to it, of course,
but it hardly helps
that this she-snake
sinks her fangs into me daily,
then hides her venom
behind the angelic
toothpaste smile
she keeps on rewind,
that just-right white
toothy grin her mother
is forever fooled by.
Desperate for a steady place
with bed and pillow,
I bite my tongue

and choke down the easy curses
I've memorized for
just such occasions.
Yeah, once in a while,
I flash like lightning,
slam doors and smash whatever
cutesy knickknacks
might be handy.
And guess who gets
to sweep up the mess?
Mostly, I march through my days,
footsteps falling on deaf ears,
even when I stomp.
If I yell for help,
no one comes,
my voice always
a lonely echo,
no matter how crowded
the room.
Even the invisible
occupy a certain space.
Me? I can't seem
to find a single place
to be seen.
To be heard.
And so I drift,
seething,
silent.
Until now.

DARRIAN

Man! No wonder that girl looks pissed half the time. Her life sounds messed up.

I thought foster kids had it better than orphans, but maybe not. I guess just because they have a place to stay doesn't make it the same as having *familia.* Me and Papi, we look out for each other. Nobody's invisible in our house. Jenesis—that's a whole other story.

GIRL MISSING IN PLAIN SIGHT

She's a kind of lonely I've never been.

We should be giving her a reason to smile. Somebody should step up. I could give it a shot.

"Hey, Jenesis," I begin. "Nice poem today."

FREDDIE HOUSTON

I'm sixteen years old and pretty much a full-time mother of two. First, there's my eight-year-old niece, Carrie, my sister's kid. Where's her mom? She's probably in a shooting gallery somewhere, plugging up her veins with heroin. Don't ask. Then there's my mother, child number two. I'd laugh if it were funny, if it weren't true, but my mother forgot how to be one the first time she brought a bottle of gin up to her lips and tried to wash away all her brain cells, leaving me on my own with the niece who needs somebody to look out for her. Tag. I'm it.

Why couldn't I just have a mom like most of the kids at school? Someone who'd take care of me, instead of the other way around?

I throw out the empty gin bottles Mom leaves all over the house when she's on one of her binges. I used to try pouring her poison down the drain, but that stopped the day she caught me tipping one of her precious bottles over the toilet bowl. She balled her fists, hauled off, and knocked me clear across the room. After that, I figured if she wanted her booze that bad, she could have it. Now I just take care of the house, try to keep the mess down to a minimum so Carrie can have a halfway-decent-looking apartment to come home to after school. Bad enough she's too ashamed to bring any of her friends here. Mom actually wonders why. She can't seem to see she's two different people: the neat and sober one who goes to work every day, and the useless alcoholic her child and grandchild get to deal with most nights.

There's not much I can do about Mom except help her to bed when she needs me to. So I focus on cooking, doing the laundry, mopping the floors, and keeping the dirty dishes from overflowing the kitchen sink. I grab money from her purse and get groceries when we run out. Mom usually manages to pay the bills on time, but I check once a week, just in case. Most nights, I squeeze in time to help Carrie with her homework, plus do my own. Hell. I get so tired.

I love it when a boy at school asks me if I want to hang, like I got time to throw away on some guy looking to party. Please!

The only kid in this class who for sure gets that life is not always a party is Jenesis. That's why we hit it off so fast. I could tell we was on the same radar. Most foster kids I've met have it rough, so it's no surprise Jenesis gets me.

When things at home get real bad, I shut my eyes, picture myself curled up on the grass of a college campus somewhere far away, book by Chaucer open on my lap, soft music pumping through my headphones. I'm soaking up all the knowledge I want, with no interruptions and no gin fumes clogging my nostrils. I feel the muscles in my jaw relax, the corners of my mouth lifting, slow and easy, into a smile. Call it a dream if you want to, but one of these days—

"Freddie!" Carrie cries out. "I'm hungry. What's for dinner?"

Eggs. Again. I don't tell Carrie that, though.

"Something yummy," I tell her.

It ain't really a lie. I'll make sure the eggs are tasty. I'm getting pretty good at coming up with different ways to make them. Not much choice, since that's all we got right now. It's the end of the month, and Mom's money don't go but so far. She should be the one trying to make the food stretch.

I don't even have to ask where Mom is. I'm willing to bet she's slung across her unmade bed, fully dressed, out cold. Again.

I should write a poem about that, huh, Mr. Ward? No. I suppose not.

I end up writing a poem with some truth tucked inside. Before it's my turn to read on Open Mike Friday for the first time, the boy sitting behind me taps me on the shoulder. I turn around to find a mouth full of teeth grinning at me.

"I don't think we've met yet. My name is Darrian. What's yours?"

I decide to be polite. "It's Freddie."

"Freddie? That's a strange name for a girl."

So much for polite. "What? You think I should maybe roll up on the Grand Concourse, calling myself Fredericka? Huh? Or you think my parents could have come up with a name you like better, something common like Jane, or Laurie, or maybe Mary Ann?"

"Well, no. I just meant–"

"The name's Freddie. Take it or leave it."

"Damn, girl. You're hard," says Darrian.

"Yeah, well, maybe there's a reason." I turn around to face front, leg bouncing nervously until Mr. Ward tells me it's my turn to step up to the microphone.

"You go, girl!" says Jenesis. And so I do.

Escape

by Freddie Houston

Come rain or shine,
escape *is a word*
I turn over like a rock
in my dreams,
wondering each time
what I might find.
I feel ready
for an adventure,
but before I can measure
the distance I want to travel,
a thin voice pleads,
"Stay! Stay!"
As I'm about to get away,
somebody catches me with cords
of love and memory,
and before I know it, I see
my suitcase unpack itself,
leaving me and my
dreams of adventure
back on the shelf
of my crazy wide-awake life.
Meanwhile, I'm still
desperate for a change of view.
I chew a fingernail until
I notice a solution
resting on the bed stand

inches from my right hand,
sitting on the pile of schoolbooks
I've never been happier to have.
I pick up the right one,
flip through its pages,
and run, run, run
as fast and far away as I can
for the night
with Shakespeare.

DARRIAN

I studied Freddie when she spoke, and when she read her poem in class. Marcel seems to be studying her, too. Her eyes are soft, even though her words are sometimes hard. She said there was a reason for that, and I believe her. You can tell just a little from her poem, but I know there's more story underneath the words, and I'll find it. I'm a newsman, after all. Or at least I plan to be. Sniffing out stories is my job. Didn't I catch Kyle giving Angela lessons on his skateboard the other day? Looks like she's hoping his fearlessness will rub off on her.

You just wait, Freddie. Give me a little time, and I'll find out what your story is.

DOGGED REPORTER DIGS UP TRUTH

I wonder what Freddie's going to write for the poetry slam. I've been reading up on slams. If I'm going to write about ours for the school paper, I should do a little research, yes? But what would really help is to actually start working on one, so this morning, I raise my hand and get Mr. Ward's attention.

"Mr. Ward, when are we going to start working on the slam?"

"The poetry slam! Yes! It is time we begin to practice. Thanks for the reminder, Darrian. Before we get into the practice schedule, though, let's go over some of the details of a poetry slam, because not all of us have been to one.

"And by the way, the poetry slam is optional. You don't have to participate if you don't want to. It's strictly your choice. Your final grade will not be affected one way or the other.

"Okay. Now, a slam is a competitive series of poetry performances. Both individual poets and poetry teams perform their poems, and a combination of judges gives each performance a score throughout the evening. The team that racks up the highest cumulative points wins. But, as those of us who love poetry like to say, the point is not the points. The point is the poetry. And so, what I really want each of you to focus on is the poetry itself. I want you to work hard on the language of your poetry, the rhythms of your poetry, and the emotional truth of your poetry.

"Now, about the practice sessions. Since we're going to have two teams, I think each should practice separately. Ladies first, so Team Girlz, you'll practice on Tuesdays. Team Boyz, you'll get together on Thursdays."

I look around the room, see everyone nodding. We're on!

"I can't wait to check out the girls," I say, grinning.

"Oh, snap! Darrian's going on Barbie Patrol!" cracks one of the boys. Freddie whips her head around, searching for the speaker. She doesn't spot him, so she cuts her eyes at all the boys in general.

"Sorry, Darrian," says Mr. Ward. "I should have explained. Those practices are to be private. Each team keeps to itself."

"But I have to cover the practices for the school paper!" I say.

"Well, you can cover Team Boyz's practices as much as you want," says Mr. Ward. "But Team Girlz is off limits to you."

"Dang!" says Kyle.

Freddie turns around and mouths, "Sorry," which I can tell she's not.

MR. KILLJOY COMES TO TOWN

I glare at Mr. Ward, but he just ignores me and asks, "Any questions?"

LI

The best thing about Saturday mornings is getting to sleep in. At least that's what my classmates tell me. I'd hardly know. I may not have Mandarin language classes on Saturdays like my other Chinese friends because my parents want me to be all-American, but that doesn't mean I get to stay in bed. My industrious mother always manages to find something for me to do just after sunrise. Today, it's cleaning bathroom tiles and polishing the faucets.

Since I'm already in the bathroom, I finish up with a quick shower, then get dressed. Before I lace up my sneakers, I think of slipping under the covers for a few more minutes of sleep.

"Li," calls my mother.

Just for a little while. A short nap.

"Li!"

"Yes, MaMa."

"I need you to run to the market for me."

So much for crawling back into bed.

"Coming, MaMa."

I find her at the kitchen table, making a list. I wait. Eventually, she hands it to me and I head out the door.

I'm so busy studying the list as I walk that I practically bump into Maylin.

"Hey! Where are you going to in such a hurry?" she asks. Hanna is with her, and so is Jing.

"Oh! Hello! Sorry I didn't see you. MaMa gave me a long list of vegetables and herbs to pick up for her. I was just checking it over."

"If your mother's got you out this early on a Saturday morning, she might as well send you to Chinese school with us!" says Jing. I've explained a hundred times why my parents chose not to send me, so I just shrug, but Hanna gives Jing a sharp look.

"What?" asks Jing. "I just think Li should have a chance to meet some of the cute boys we have in Chinese school."

"She already has a boyfriend, remember?" teases Hanna. "His name is Darrian, right?"

I study my sneakers.

"Yes," says Jing, "but she should meet Henry Wong."

"Ha!" says Maylin, and she and Jing slip easily into Mandarin for a minute, sharing a story that leaves Hanna in giggles.

I look back and forth from one to the other.

"What?" I ask. "What's so funny?"

"Oh! Sorry," says Maylin, realizing she'd switched languages. "It was just something silly about Henry. He has a crush on Hanna, who won't even give him the time of day. But poor Henry follows Hanna around like a puppy."

"That's sad," I say.

"I know," says Maylin.

"Yes," agrees Jing, "but it's kind of funny, too." Jing laughs again, very loudly.

"Shh! Not so loud," says Maylin.

Jing rolls her eyes. "What? Did I wake the ancestors? Again? You know me. I was born loud."

"Please!" Maylin smiles at an old woman passing by as if to apologize for her noisy friend.

"Okay. Okay!" Jing lowers her voice. "Sorry."

"We have to go or we'll be late," says Hanna. She grabs Maylin by the hand and tugs her to follow.

I wave goodbye to the club of three. The club that doesn't include me.

I think about Val's immigrant parents. Maybe one day I'll tell her there's more than one way to feel like an alien.

All-American

from Li's notebook

I envy the easy laughter
of my Chinese friends,
using their well-trained tongues
to share stories
in a language
withheld from me
like a secret.
My well-meaning parents
have left me jealous
of every ni hao ma, *every* zai jian
that falls from lips
which look like mine
but aren't.
Lonely is my
perfectly enunciated
all-American English.
I sometimes wish
I didn't understand
the mathematics
of being different.

MARCEL

I wake up this morning, find Pops slung across a kitchen chair, throwing back a beer. The table is a mess of empty cans, some crushed, some bent in the middle. I go to pick up the empties and throw them away, but Pops snaps.

"Leave 'em! Leave 'em right there. I don't need you picking up after me, boy. You think I can't do it?"

"No. It's not that, Pops. I just thought–"

"You thought what?" he snarls.

"Nothing, Pops," I say.

"You think your old man is useless now, just 'cause he can't get a decent job?"

I shake my head and look away. No point in speaking. There ain't no right thing to say to Pops these days, no vocabulary that's gonna take away his pain.

I miss my dad. I wish the kids at school could've met him.

School. I love how everyone there talks about truth, like it's one thing and everybody agrees on it. But it's not. And even if it is, some people treat it like it doesn't matter worth a damn.

My pops got swept up in one those neighborhood war-on-drugs raids that keep hitting the hood. What? You think it's an accident that 80 to 90 percent of all drug offenders are Black or Brown? Please.

Tyrone gets it. Darrian, too. They've been hassled by cops as often as me. You just be walking down the street while Black or Brown, and next thing you know, you're shoved up against the wall, explaining that you're just minding your business, trying to get home, and you don't know nothing about no kid selling drugs on the corner or whatever. And you turn your pockets inside out quick, before that cop has a chance to sneak a nickel bag on you so he can set you up for an arrest to make his quota. Just ask me. Just ask my father.

Pops was on his way home from work one day when I was twelve. He's minding his own business, coming down the street. I see him from the stoop and wave. That's when a row of cop cars pile into our street. Dad looks around but doesn't seem worried. Why should he? He hasn't done anything. Besides, he's got on his MTA uniform, and he wears it likes it's armor. Who's gonna give him grief when they see he's a man in uniform? So he keeps walking straight ahead, his eyes on mine.

He lifts his arm to wave at me, and blue suits start spilling from their cars, slamming people against the wall, left and right.

"Dad!" I call out. I'm frozen at the top of the stoop, but I'm watching everything. A policeman grabs Pops and gives him a shove.

"Over there!" he orders, motioning to the growing line of guys against an apartment wall.

"Excuse me, Officer," says Pops, "but I'm not–"

The policeman twists his arm. "Did I ask you to speak?"

Pops tries again. "Officer, there has been some–"

The blue suit jabs Pops with his nightstick. "Shut the f– up and get over there with your buddies. Now!" growls the officer.

"Pops!" I scream.

Pops closes his mouth and does as he is told. Even from where I am, I can see his shoulders start to slump. It's when the handcuffs are put on my father that I lose it.

"No!" I scream, and take off down the stairs. Just as I reach the bottom step, Mom grabs me from behind. She must have come out when she heard all the sirens.

"Let me go!" I tell her, struggling against arms that are suddenly made of steel.

"You stay put, Marcel," she orders.

"But Pops–"

"I know, son. I know. But I can't let you get in the middle of this. We've just got to wait. It's gonna be all right. They'll see that your father is a good working man who hasn't done anything wrong, and they'll let him go. You'll see. Hush, now."

She keeps saying, "Shush. Hush now, baby," even after Pops is loaded into a police car. Even after that car carries him away.

They say when you see a policeman, don't run. Why run if you're innocent? So my pops didn't run. A lot of good that did him.

Everyone arrested that night went to jail. After a week,

my father's court-appointed attorney told him to plead guilty to drug distribution, even though Pops was innocent. Lawyer told him the prosecutor was offering probation. But that's crazy, 'cause my pops is innocent! He had the truth on his side, right? Nobody was interested in the truth, though. Nobody cared that he worked for the MTA. Nobody cared that he didn't do drugs or sell them. He was "caught" in a drug sweep, so he was guilty until somebody important decided different. After a month of missing his family, and missing his job, and missing his bed, he agreed to the plea so that he could go home. They slapped him with ten years' probation, plus fines. Then they set him free.

Free, my ass. The pops I knew is still locked up inside. He never did come home.

And guess what. That judge eventually dismissed the cases against everyone else in that group who didn't plead guilty like Pops. There were only a few. Lucky for them. Turns out the arrest was based on the word of some lying rat who wanted to cut a deal with the prosecutor to shorten his own prison sentence. You think my dad's court-appointed attorney knew or cared about that? He didn't even stick around long enough to find out.

Go ahead. Ask me one more time why I'm mad as hell. I dare you.

Maybe it's time I take the mike in Mr. Ward's class, give everyone the real 411 on the war on drugs.

Sweep

by Marcel Dixon

Sweep. *That's a good word,*
the way cops roll up on the hood,
treating Black boys, Black men
like dirt.
That's what you sweep up, right?
I've seen them swoop in,
billy clubs swinging–
the only kind of brooms they need
to gather up any bodies
unlucky enough to be
at the wrong place
at the wrong time
like my dad.
Too bad
so sad
your dad got busted
in a war he never
enlisted in.
I watched his face
get shoved to the ground,
never mind that no drugs
were ever found
on his person.
He is a person, remember?
Did they?
Either way, his arrest

was hardly what you'd call
a waste.
After all,
it did help one cop
make his quota
for the night.

DARRIAN

Damn.

BLACK BROTHER BREAKS IT DOWN

I sit with Marcel's poem for a minute, think about my cousin Javier, who we called Giant because, at six feet, he was the biggest man in our family. I think about how he got snatched up one day on a corner where somebody was selling coke. Cops didn't even give him a chance to explain that he was only passing by. They just shoved him in the back of their car, hauled him off to jail, and disappeared him from our lives.

Bam! Just like that.

Marcel's words took me there, to that moment. The anger I felt as a little boy watching my big cousin being slammed against the car, then handcuffed; his helplessness and mine; the hurt that was more than enough to go around. I remember the hot tears streaking down my face. I feel them trying to come again.

I breathe heavy, push down the thoughts, unclench my fists, shake my head to clear it.

"Good," says Mr. Ward, suddenly standing over my

desk. "You're learning how powerful poetry can be. Think about how the right use of words can shape the stories you want to write. Think about how you can use this tool to impact the people who will read those stories. Think about that."

I close my eyes for a minute and concentrate on his words, think about all the things Marcel's poem made me feel.

He's right. If I can put words together in a way that can make somebody tremble inside, or cry, or maybe even clench their fists long enough to feel their anger, then let it go—that's a good thing, a good tool. I just have to be careful how I use it.

I open my eyes and Mr. Ward's still standing there. I give him a nod. He reaches down, gives my shoulder a squeeze.

"Keep sharpening your tools, Darrian. One day, they will serve you well."

"Thanks, Mr. Ward," I say.

BOY GOES BACK TO THE TOOLSHED

LI

I have study hall this period, one of my favorite times of the day. Most of my classmates use the time to catch up on schoolwork. But of course, I'm never behind, so I go to the library and use the time to write poetry. Not for class, just for myself.

Can you imagine if I was ever actually behind in my schoolwork? My mother would sprout a second head and the mouths of both of them would shout at me.

"Li Hsu Cheng!" She uses my whole name when she's angry. "How do you expect to get into Princeton or Yale if you don't study? I do not give you permission to waste your brain!" I would never hear the end of it, so I don't give my mother an excuse to start.

I mentioned the poetry slam to my parents, but I just called it a poetry reading. A slam isn't something they would understand.

"Why do you have to do a poetry reading?" asked my father.

"I don't have to, BaBa," I said. "I want to."

My father shook his head. "Well, as long as it does not interfere with your studies."

"It won't," I said. That seemed to satisfy both parents. Thankfully, the subject was dropped.

When I reach the library, I settle at a quiet table at the end of the poetry section and open my journal. I've been reading a lot of contemporary Chinese poetry lately, finding so many perfect lines by William Marr and others. Ah Xin writes, "Dawn, dripping with dew, floats down to the grassland at the foothills, like an armada." Chen Yanqiang's verses are no less sweet: "Right now, the night is getting deeper / and feeling even quieter than my loneliness." It is Li Li, though, who reads my mind: "Let me count a few things that I can't do without. . . . the lovely words on the pages I turn." Of course we have the same name, but Li and I also have the same heart!

I'm not just reading contemporary poetry, though. I'm also studying classical forms like tanka, which I really like. I want to try writing a few of my own. I bite the end of my pen while I decide on the opening line and mentally count out the syllables. The first five come easily: *More than metaphor.* That's as far as I get.

"Hello!"

I look up to find Darrian grinning at me.

"I came here to work on my poem for class. Do you mind?"

Before I can answer, he pulls up the chair opposite me and plops down.

Great. Now how am I supposed to concentrate? I lower my eyes to at least try.

"You're really good at this poetry stuff," says Darrian. He leans toward me so he doesn't have to speak too loudly. He doesn't want to disturb the other readers. Just me.

"Well, I love poetry, so I read a lot of it."

"And write it."

"Yes. And write it."

Now will you please leave me alone? I can't concentrate with you here.

I drop my head and focus on the page in front of me, and try to pick up the poem from where I started. I bring my pen to the page, and–

"Since you're so good at poetry," says Darrian, "and I'm only beginning, I wonder if you could help me."

I sigh and set my pen down on the table.

I tighten my ponytail and ignore my rapid heartbeat. "Okay. I don't know how I can help you," I say, "but I'll try."

Darrian's eyes twinkle.

"Great! I mean, thank you." Darrian clears his throat and puts on a serious face. "Well, to begin, maybe you could tell me what you love about poetry, just so I understand. I really think that would help me."

I don't see how answering this question will help him, but I suppose it won't hurt.

"Most writing is sharing information. The information may be interesting, but the writing usually isn't. It's . . . flat. But poetry! Poetry sings, and that's what I love, the way you can weave words together so they make music and practically dance across the page. Sometimes I read a poem and the words are so delicious, I want to spoon them onto a dish and eat them for dinner."

"Dancing and delicious?" Darrian looks confused.

"Okay. I'm mixing metaphors, but this is hard to explain. It's really all about the words. I love language. I love the way each word feels differently on the tongue, and how each one sounds. And poetry takes advantage of that."

"Now, that makes sense. Not the singing, but about each word being unique, special. I love newspaper writing, especially headlines. A good headline only has a few words, but if you choose the right ones, a headline reveals the heart of the story."

"You're right!" I say. "I never thought about that."

"And a newspaper story, well, it might not sing," says Darrian, "but it can be beautiful, especially if it's true."

"That's something poetry and newspapers have in common, then. Truth. A poem that is not true is simply a manipulation of beauty."

"A beautiful lie," says Darrian.

"Yes."

"A rip-off."

"Yes!"

Darrian and I both smile.

"And when a story is true, you have to tell it, and you have to write it in a way that will force people to stop and read it. That's when choosing the right word matters most. When the story the ink is printing on the page is true, the words have to be—"

"Perfect?"

"Exactly!" says Darrian.

I never get around to my tanka poems. Instead, Darrian and I spend the hour talking. He shows me his notebook of story ideas and headlines, and I share a few of my personal poems.

When the change bell rings, we rush off to our next classes, knowing we'll speak together again. Soon.

Wild Words

by Li Cheng

Words
crack me open.
Only the right ones, of course,
those laced with beauty
or infused with the sweetness
of a ripe peach.
Each word, each lyrical phrase,
often powerful enough
to break, or heal,
the heart.
But you knew this
from the start.
Why else would you
come offering to share
your own wild words
with plain, ordinary me*?*
Words are clearly
the truest thing
we have in common.
Still, why me?
Never mind.
Your clever lines
have lassoed
my attention.
I'm listening.

DARRIAN

I casually look around the classroom, try to see if anyone has read between the lines. No one is looking in my direction, so I guess Li's poem about me, about us, is still our secret.

Bueno.

Of course, I think her poem is perfection. Still, something tells me she won't be saving that poem for the slam.

POEM PADLOCKS BUDDING RELATIONSHIP

On the way to lunch, I think about asking Li for a copy of that poem, but I get sidetracked. Some White kids I don't know are jawing about Marcel. One of them gives him a nasty look and says, loud enough for him to hear, "There goes our junior felon. Or is it Felon Junior?"

Marcel spins around and cuts the kid up with a look that says, *You really don't want to mess with me,* and the kid takes off.

"Yo, Marcel," I call. "Wait up."

When I get close enough, I say, "Hey, man. Why don't you come sit with me at lunch."

"I'm not that hungry," he says.

I figure it's that stupid comment that has spoiled his appetite.

"Look, blood," I tell him, "don't even pay that fool any attention. What does he know about being pulled over just 'cause your skin's the wrong color? And don't even get me started on that so-called war on drugs designed to destroy my people and yours. I guarantee you he don't know squat about that!"

"Naw, man," says Marcel. "It ain't that. I don't care about that dude. I just thought I'd drop in on the gym while it's empty and shoot a few hoops for a minute. Try to keep my mind off of stuff."

I'm not stupid. I don't ask him what "stuff."

"Okay. Well, later, man." I'm about to walk away when Marcel starts talking.

"I'm just feelin' a little off," he says. "Today's the anniversary of the night my pops got arrested and my family got split wide open, our guts spilling everywhere."

I wait for him to say more, but he doesn't.

"That's rough, man." I know that sounds lame, but what else can I say? I heard Mr. Ward say something once that fits: *Words are powerful, but sometimes words have a limit.*

I decide to skip lunch and join Marcel in the gym. Mr. Hunt, the assistant principal, sees us slip in.

"You know you're not supposed to be in here now," he says. We need to be here, though, and he can tell.

"Just keep the door open," he says. "I'll come back and check on you in a few minutes."

"Thanks," I say, for both of us.

Marcel dunks the ball a bunch of times, and then we run it up and down the court, taking turns going to the net. I hit the rim more often than I score, but I'm only half trying. Truth is, my stomach's growling. Marcel's another story. I think he meant it when he said he wasn't hungry. He's too busy working something out. You can tell because Marcel is dribbling that ball so hard, I swear the floor's about to crack.

BOY BEATS GYM FLOORBOARDS TO BITS

Seriously.

When the change bell rings, all I can think is *Thank God.* One, I get to go to my locker and grab the leftover piece of chocolate bar stuffed in my backpack from yesterday, and two, I get some distance from Anger Boy.

"Take care, Marcel," I say, and I'm gone.

TEAM GIRLZ: **ANGELA**

Only four of us made it for the first meeting: me, Jenesis, Freddie, and Val. I wish she would let us call her Valentina. It's such a beautiful name.

Freddie came in late, out of breath. She said something about running home to get her niece settled in with a neighbor. We had to wait for Mr. Ward to finish grading papers before we could get started anyway, so it turns out Freddie had plenty of time to get home and back.

I had asked Li to come with me, but she's taking the SAT early. They're offering it this weekend, and she said she needs to study. Yeah. Like there's any chance she won't ace it. She could do that test in her sleep.

"But it'll be fun!" I told Li. "Can't you skip the test, do it another day?"

"Sorry. I can't. But I'll make it to the next rehearsal, I promise," she said so I wouldn't push.

I don't plan on doing much talking at this rehearsal. I'll just watch, see how it goes. I don't know anything about poetry slams. I don't even know anybody who knows anything about poetry slams. Besides, the idea of being in one makes me nervous. What if I get up to do my poem and I blank out again, like I did that first time? The whole thing is scary.

We all take our usual seats and wait. It seems like forever before Mr. Ward looks up from his desk. He stacks his papers, sets them aside, and smiles.

"Anyone in the mood for a little poetry tonight?" He doesn't wait for us to answer, he just jumps up and arranges a few chairs in an open circle. We each take a seat and wait to see who's going to speak first. Naturally, it's Mr. Ward.

"Welcome, Team Girlz! Since this is a new experience for most of you, I think a great way to get started is to break the ice and get to know each other a little bit. And my favorite icebreaker is a free write."

I slip my hand up as if we're in Language Arts.

"You don't have to raise your hand, Angela," says Jenesis. Embarrassed, I let my arm drop.

"What's a free–what did you call it?"

"A free write," said Mr. Ward.

"Yeah. That. What is it?"

"Actually, it's exactly what it sounds like. I give you all the same subject to write about, and for a few minutes, you are free to write whatever you want to about that subject. The idea is to keep your pen on the page, writing continuously, until the time is up. You write whatever comes to your mind without worrying about grammar, or what others will think. Just write with no constraints except time. Write freely. Then, once everyone is done, each of you will share whatever you've written with one another."

Why did he have to mention sharing? Everything was fine until he mentioned sharing. God! Why did I sign up for this?

"So, what's the subject?" asks Freddie. Mr. Ward smiles.

"Scars," he says.

"Scars," Freddie repeats.

"Yes. Scars. It can be a physical scar or an emotional scar. You choose," says Mr. Ward.

"Got it," says Freddie.

Mr. Ward claps his hands. "Okay! Take out your notebooks and get started. I'll give you, let's see—five minutes. And your time starts . . . Angela, where's your notebook?"

I quickly rummage through my backpack and pull out a pen and my spiral notebook.

"Ready?" asks Mr. Ward.

I nod.

"Your five minutes starts now!"

"Well, here goes nothing," I whisper. Val catches my eye and nods for me to begin.

> *The first scar I think of is the one on my right leg. I was seven or eight years old, and just getting comfortable riding a two-wheeler, and I rode up and down the street for no reason except to feel the wind on my face, and this one time, I decided to take my hands off of the handlebar, like I'd seen some of the older kids do, and my mother had just come outside to check the mailbox, and I turned my head toward her, grinning proudly, and said, "Look, Ma! No hands!" and ran right off the curb, flipped over,*

and came away with a bloody gash across my right leg.

I'd never seen that much blood in my life before, except on TV, and for a while there, I didn't know if it was ever going to stop. But it wasn't the fall, or the blood, that scared me. It was that I was so sure that I could ride a bike perfectly, only I couldn't. And it made me wonder what else I thought I could do, but really couldn't. Up till then, I always thought I had it in me to do anything, to try anything, to be anything. Suddenly, I wasn't so sure.

That's the day I started being afraid!

Now I hold myself back from trying anything new, anything risky–and not just physically–because, who knows? I might get my heart broken, or my feelings hurt, or get embarrassed, or get my body banged up and bloody again–as if getting banged up is the worst thing in the world! After Kyle tells me, over lunch one day, about all his different surgeries, and his heart nearly stopping, I know better.

Suddenly, Mr. Ward is yelling, "Time!" We all look up, startled. I think everybody could've kept writing.

I look across at Freddie, Jenesis, and Val, and they all have that faraway look, like they just got back from a long journey, which is exactly how I feel.

"Okay," says Mr. Ward. "Who wants to read first?"

I slip my hand up. "I'll go," I say, and for the first time in a long time, I don't feel afraid. Not even a little.

Jenesis goes next, then Val. Freddie reads last. When she finishes, Mr. Ward gives us a huge smile.

"Now," he says, "you've all got something to write a poem about. Great start, ladies."

JENESIS

Val leaves right after the free write, but the rest of us hang around for a minute. While Mr. Ward packs up his satchel, Freddie and I pull Angela aside.

"I liked your free write," I tell her.

"Thanks."

"You know, there's lots of things to be afraid of in life. The trick is not to let that fear get in the way of what you want."

"Preach!" says Freddie.

"You've got to take that fear and show it who's boss, okay?"

Angela nods. "I think I did that today," she says.

"You damn sure did," says Freddie.

Angela smiles. Next thing I know, she's throwing her arms around Freddie and me and hugging us like we're her long-lost cousins.

"Thank you," she whispers. Then she grabs her notebook and runs out the door.

Jenesis and I look at each other and laugh.

"That was weird," I say.

"Tell me about it," says Freddie. "Her free write was really good, though."

"Yeah," says Jenesis. "She owned it. And for once, there was no fear in her eyes."

FREDDIE

We had to write an essay this week, and Angela came up with this dog-ate-my-homework excuse for not turning hers in on time. Seriously. I just shook my head.

Why is no one else bothered by Little Miss Redhead? So she's got a phobia or two. Big whoop. She can afford to see a shrink about it, she's got Hollywood looks, both parents, a room in a house her parents own, and nobody to look after but herself, so from where I stand, her life looks pretty perfect.

She should try trading places with Jenesis, or with me.

You want to talk excuses? You want to talk real issues? Fine. I'll go first.

Last night, Carrie was in the mood for attention—like I actually had time to give her some. And, of course, Mom was missing in action.

I made Carrie some macaroni and cheese for dinner and went to my room to get some homework done while she ate. But thirty seconds after I cracked my book open, she was screaming for me to come sit with her, 'cause all of a sudden she couldn't eat by herself. Fine. I went to sit with her, anything to spare my eardrums. After the mess of dinner (how exactly did that glob of macaroni end up on the wall?), I got her settled in front of the TV and went back to my room.

"Aunt Freddie!" Carrie yelled for me. "Aunt Freddie! AUNT FREDDIE!"

There was absolutely nothing wrong with that girl, and I knew it, so I closed my door and turned to my homework assignment.

It took me a minute to clear my mind. I shook out thoughts of my deadbeat sister, my missing mother, my screaming niece, who's got every right to want somebody to pay attention to her, and I forced myself to focus on the subject. I picked up my pen to write, and three words into the first sentence, the volume of the TV was cranked up so high, the walls vibrated.

"Damn it, Carrie!"

I stomped down the hall into the living room, grabbed Carrie's arm, and squeezed. She looked up at me, wide eyed, too scared to do more than whimper. Suddenly, I was five years old, and my mom, half drunk or angry or both, slammed me across a room. I banged against the wall and looked up at her the same way Carrie looked at me. I started to shiver and dropped Carrie's arm.

"I'm sorry," I whispered. "I'm so sorry, Carrie." And I took her in my arms and rocked her for a long while. Then I set her down on the sofa and sat next to her to keep her company. I leaned my head back on the sofa, let Carrie watch TV, and quietly waited until it was her bedtime.

After I tucked Carrie in for the night, I went to the living room, curled up on the sofa, and tried to quiet myself.

My niece. She's driving me crazy, I swear. Sometimes I feel like I could really hurt her. When I squeezed Carrie's arm so tight, it scared her. Scared me, too.

I counted to ten, breathed, tried to get myself in control.

Lord, don't let me hurt that child. Please.

A voice inside me said, *Just love her the best you can.*

I took another deep breath and went to Mom's room, got her out of her clothes, and helped her into bed. I smoothed her hair away from her face and kissed her forehead.

It was late when I finally got back to working on my assignment.

I was up for hours, but I got my essay done. So it ticks me off when kids come to class with those dog-ate-my-homework stories. And it really fries me when the teacher buys it.

But Mr. Ward's not buying Angela's story this morning.

"I expect that essay tomorrow, Angela," says Mr. Ward. "No more excuses."

"Yes, Mr. Ward," mumbles Angela.

That makes me smile.

"From now on," adds Mr. Ward, "anyone who fails to turn in assignments on time will be excluded from the poetry slam. It's your choice."

That's not even funny. We're just starting to get a rhythm going, and Angela's part of that. She better get her act together, is all I'm saying. I give her a look that says so. She sets her jaw tight, so I know she's taking this seriously. Good.

No Excuses

by Freddie Houston

People tell me
I have a penchant
for speaking my mind,
so maybe it's about time
I tell you something:
I have zero patience
for the excuses
a few people parade
in place of whatever
homework assignment
is due. You
would have to go
to hell and back
in order to beat me
for rational reasons
to miss a deadline,
except I'm not inclined
to use any.
Look here:
I was born into a world
of narrow spaces.
Every breath I take
is dedicated to pressing
back the walls,
forcing them to move
by the sheer strength

of my stubbornness.
The mathematics of poverty
are already against me,
so I allow no wiggle room
for excuses.
You feel me?
I will, I will, I will
break into a world
large enough to contain
all that I am
capable of doing,
capable of being.
And not a single excuse
will get in my way.
I wonder:
Can you say
the same?

TEAM BOYZ: **DARRIAN**

The girls are mum. I haven't been able to get a word out of them about their slam practice, not even from Li, and she's my little honey. Whoever said girls like to run off at the mouth hasn't met these *chicas*!

SECRETS UNDER LOCK AND KEY

I don't know why they call women the weaker sex. I don't see any weakness here. Papi says girls are born knowing how to balance the world on one hip. Boys, we're still trying to figure out how. We just don't admit it. I think Papi's right.

So now it's our turn, and Mr. Ward starts us off with something called a free write. He tells us to write whatever we want for five minutes.

"Write about what?" I ask him.

"Guilt," he says.

I shiver. I know about guilt. Every time I think about Mami and the last time I saw her, guilt takes a chunk out of me. Even though Papi says I shouldn't feel that way.

Mr. Ward says, "Go," and my hand moves across the page like it's been waiting for this chance.

I can't stand the smell of hospitals, or that endless beep, beep, beeping of those machines hooked up to people who look half dead already. Mami was half dead. Maybe even three-quarters, but she kept hanging on, mostly because we wanted her to. But what was the point? The cancer had already won. Mami was mostly bones, and her skin–you could practically see through it. And no hair. She had no hair left.

Where'd my beautiful Mami go?

One afternoon, I just couldn't just sit there anymore, next to that cold metal hospital bed, waiting for her to–

I ran out of the room, told Papi I needed a soda. Told him I'd be right back. But I wasn't. I pushed through the hospital doors, stumbled outside, and gulped as much air as my lungs could take. I started walking, first just up the block and back again. Then I walked around the block, and crossed Broadway, and kept walking, walking, not paying attention to where I was or how much time had passed.

Why? Why did my mother have to get cancer? It wasn't enough that she was poor all her life? That she worked herself to the bone? That she hardly had time to spend with her family, with me? God, you're making a big mistake. Take somebody else. Please!

I don't know when I started crying. Eventually, I went back to the hospital to sit with Papi. But it was too late. Mami was already gone. How many times can you say I'm sorry? It seems like that's all

I could think of to say to Papi. I wasn't there in the end. I wasn't there to say goodbye, to tell Mami I love her. I love you, Mami! I'm sorry I wasn't there to say goodbye. Please forgive me. I don't want to feel guilty anymore.

"Time!" calls Mr. Ward.

I had forgotten he was there. I had forgotten the other boys were there, too.

I wipe my face with the back of my hand, and cough a few times to clear my throat.

"Okay," says Mr. Ward. "Who wants to share first?"

On the way home, I spot Zeke and Shorty at the neighborhood basketball court. Zeke's doing his best impression of Kobe Bryant going for a layup, but he fumbles the ball.

"Man, this is painful! Give. It. Up," taunts Shorty from the bench.

"Shut it!" says Zeke. He chases the ball, dribbles it up to the basket, then notices me.

"Yo!" he calls out. "Wazzup?"

"Hey," I manage, but I keep walking. I'm in no mood to watch Zeke practice shots or to sit around with Shorty jawing about his dreams, or even mine. Not tonight. I just want to be quiet. I just want to sit with my thoughts about Mami.

Private Pain

by Darrian Lopez

Numb, I sit on the edge
of the bed
Mami y *Papi share.*
Shared.
I feel light as the ghost
my mother has become.
Her picture
on the bedside table
looks blurry until
I wipe my eyes.
"Pobrecito," *she would say*
if she were here,
if she were anywhere
in this world.
"Mijo," *she would whisper*
and touch my cheek,
and I would answer,
"Mami."
But this time,
The word never leaves
my throat.
And what difference
does that make?
When I wasn't looking,
Mami's heart stopped
like a broken clock.

Half past 36,
the final tick,
the final tock.
Explain to me
exactly how
I'm supposed to
tell time now.

VAL

On the way home today, I pass a local bodega made ugly by a sign spray-painted across the front window: GO BACK HOME! The criminal didn't add *We don't want you here*, but he might as well have.

I want to cry, but I'm way too pissed off. The lovely old couple that run the store are as sweet as the *churros* they sell. So kind. Never hurt anyone. This country needs more people like them, not less. Fewer. Whatever.

Honestly, I don't know their story. Green card, no green card? It's none of my business. But I know they've made a home here for forever. I've seen their children, their grandbabies. They've been here for as long as I can remember.

These mean messages are turning up everywhere these days. It's crazy. Most of the people in my neighborhood were born here, but nobody asks. Go back home? We are home. There is no "back." There is only here. And we are staying. Get used to it.

Home

by Val Alvarez

Lately, I keep seeing
signs in my neighborhood
instructing me
to go back home.
Since I am home already,
apparently some definition
is required.
Home: village, house,
social unit formed by family
living together.
Place of residence.
A congenial environment where
I lay my head.
Is any of this ringing a bell?
A place of origin, as in
where a person was born,
that person being me.
Do you see what I'm getting at?
I could make it plainer,
but I'm not that sure
you're paying attention.
How about: base of operations?
Habitat. Location. Station.
Nation of which I am
a citizen, by birth,
not accident,

in case you
were wondering.
¿Entiendes? *No?*
How about this:
Americano,
su casa es mi casa.
Sorry if that rocks your boat.
Chances are,
it was leaking, anyway.

DARRIAN

I go up to Valentina as soon as she sits back down.

"Cousin," I whisper, "you have got to include that poem in the slam!"

She nods. "Okay. I was thinking about it, anyway."

"Good."

HOME, SWEET CASA: SECOND-GENERATION LATINA STAKES HER CLAIM

MARCEL

I've had my eye on Freddie for a while. She's tough. Like me. I like that.

I've been wanting to talk to her. You know. To maybe get something going. I just don't know how to start. My sister Mikayla says I've got no game, and she's right.

One day, I'm studying Freddie's hips as she moves down the school hall, heading to her next class, and it hits me: This girl is all kinds of fine. If I don't make some kind of move, somebody else will. So I go for it.

I catch up to her and say, "So, how long you been taking care of your niece?"

Freddie stops dead in her tracks, plants a hand on her hip, and cocks her head to the side. "Well, hello to you, too!"

My palms suddenly feel sweaty.

"I'm sorry. I didn't mean—" *Jeez! That sounded stupid!* "Hi. I'm Marcel."

"I know who you are," says Freddie. "We've been in the same class for weeks."

"Yeah. Yeah, but we've never, you know—talked."

Freddie drops her hand to her side, and she smiles, just a little.

"You're not good at this, are you?"

I breathe heavy. "No," I say.

That's when her smile gets big. She nods like she's made up her mind about me.

"Okay," she says. "I've been taking care of Carrie—that's my niece—since she was about two. That's when her drug-addict mom dropped her off at our house and kept going."

"Jeez," I say. "And the father?"

"Please!" says Freddie. "We don't even know who that is."

I look off for a minute, thinking about my own pops. "Maybe the kid's better off. There's all kinds of ways to lose a daddy."

"True," says Freddie. "Sometimes divorce takes him away. Other times, jail."

I don't say anything.

"At least you got yours back," says Freddie.

"Naw," I tell her.

"But didn't he get out of jail?"

"Yeah. But the guy that came back, he's not the same, you know? He's somebody altogether different."

Now Freddie's the one with no words.

The final change bell rings.

"Look," says Freddie, "we need to get out of this hall. I've got a class to get to, and so do you."

"Oh!" I say. "Right! So, uhm, I guess—"

"I'll see you later," Freddie fills in.

"Right," I say. "See ya."

I'm grinning now, 'cause that went better than I thought.

Finesse

by Marcel Dixon

Finesse is something
I should maybe
take lessons in.
I don't know.
Is there a school
where I could go,
pick up some juicy
pickup lines
to snag the attention
of a fine mama?
Or maybe it's better
to just jump in
using whatever words
gather on your tongue
like soldiers,
ready to march
as soon as you
give the order,
which is whenever
you get it in your mind
to speak.
Does it really matter
whether what comes out
makes you sound like a geek,
or just plain silly?

Who cares when you're there
in the moment,
and the mama is willing
and waiting to hear
whatever words
you're ready to throw down?
Be a clown
if you have to–
assuming
she's worth it.

DARRIAN

BROTHER EXCAVATES ENGLISH TO WIN A HOT HONEY

We all know who Marcel is talking about. It's not like he's smooth enough to hide it.

I've been meaning to call Freddie—not to cut in on Marcel, but to get her story.

I get her home phone number from the slam poets list Mr. Ward put together, and I ring her up, you know, kind of casual. She answers the phone, all business.

"Houston residence. May I help you?"

"Listen to you!" I say. "All official."

"Darrian?"

"Yeah. It's me," I say. "Good evening. See? I can be official sounding, too."

Silence.

"So, how are you this fine evening?"

"Fine. But I'm kind of— No, Carrie! Don't touch that!"

I hear a little girl's voice in the background.

"Sorry," says Freddie.

"Is that your niece?"

"You and Marcel been talking?"

"What?"

"Never mind," says Freddie. "Yeah. That's my sister's kid. Carrie."

"Cute name."

"So, Darrian? Was there something you needed?"

"No. I just wanted to talk."

"Are you serious? I need to get dinner on and help Carrie with her homework."

"You finished your poem already, I guess."

"Freddie!" This time, the voice is a woman's. "Freddie, give me a hand. I need some help."

"Coming, Mom!" yells Freddie. "Now, what was that?" she says to me.

"I was wondering if you already wrote your poem for Open Mike."

Freddie lets out a dry laugh. "No. I'll get to that after dinner, and Carrie's homework."

"FREDDIE!"

"And helping my mother with–whatever. Coming, Mom!" Freddie shouts back. "Give me a minute, Darrian."

She puts the phone down. Two minutes later, she's back.

"Sorry about that."

I whistle. "Damn, *chica.* You've got a lot on your plate."

A heavy sigh makes it all the way through the phone lines.

"Listen, Darrian, I've gotta book."

"Yeah, okay. No problem."

"Thanks for calling, though. I don't hear much from kids at school. It's not like I have time to hang out."

"I hear you," I say. "I'll see you on Friday, right?"

"Right!"

"Can't wait to hear your new piece."

"Right. Okay. Bye, then."

"*Adiós, chica.*"

I hang up the phone, shaking my head.

Man. You never know about a person, what kind of load they're carrying. No wonder she comes off hard. Who wouldn't?

GIRL ATLAS BALANCES A WORLD

TEAM GIRLZ: **FREDDIE**

School rules. That's what Mr. Ward says we have to stick to for the slam. No language. In other words, keep it clean. That works for me, since I usually have to bring my niece to after-school rehearsals. What else can I do? I've got a neighbor I can sometimes leave her with, but I don't want to make a habit of that.

I make it to rehearsal every week now. Of course, I'm usually late, blowing into the room as if the wind is giving me a push. I send Carrie to the bathroom and tell her to come right back.

"There she is. Late. Again," says Val. Angela doesn't say anything, but she shakes her head from side to side, her way of letting me know she's annoyed.

"Sorry," I say.

"Why are you always getting here late?" asks Val. "Everybody else manages to get here on time."

"I said I'm sorry."

"We get that you have to pick up Carrie first," says Angela, "but still."

"Look," I say. "There's more to it than—"

Val cuts me off. "I hate it when people are late!"

“My father says it’s disrespectful when people are late, and he’s right,” Li adds.

“Leave her alone,” says Jenesis.

“Stay out of this,” says Val.

“You don’t get it,” I say. “Sometimes, when I get home, my mom is–”

“You think you’re something special?” asks Val, all wound up. “You think we should be happy to wait on you, like we don’t all have things to do?”

“Stop it, Val!” says Jenesis. That’s when Val turns on her.

“Why the hell are you defending Freddie?” asks Val. “She’s disrespecting you, too!”

That’s it! “Hey!” I explode. “I don’t need this crap! I got enough to deal with at home. My mom came home drunk. Again. I had to put her in bed and fix dinner for when she finally wakes up. Then I had to get Carrie ready to bring her, because I can’t leave her at home when Mom is drunk, because, honestly, that’s worse than leaving her alone, so it took me a minute to get my act together and head over here. But you know what? That’s not your problem, so forget it. I’m outta here.”

I tear out of the class just as Carrie returns from the bathroom. My heart is pumping like crazy, and I lean against the wall to catch my breath, and that’s when the tears come. Carrie tugs my jacket.

“Aunt Freddie? What’s wrong?”

Angela follows me out into the hall. She tries to put her arms around me, but I push her away.

"Don't! Don't you dare go feeling sorry for me," I tell her. But Angela hugs me anyway. Then I see Li, Val, and Jenesis, and before I know it, there are arms everywhere, hugging on me and talking to me softly. Val's is the first voice I hear.

"I'm sorry, Freddie," she whispers. "I had no idea."

"Maybe I should just drop out of the slam altogether," I whisper.

"No, don't do that, sis," says Jenesis. "It's gonna be okay."

Little by little, my breathing slows.

"Please stop crying, Freddie," whispers Li. "We're here for you."

And you know what? In that moment, I believe them.

Somebody hands me a tissue. I wipe away the tears and we go back into the room.

"Is everything okay, ladies?" asks Mr. Ward. Everyone looks at me, and I nod.

"We're good," says Jenesis, speaking for all of us.

Mr. Ward looks from one of us to the other.

"I sense there's something deeply personal going on between you, and that's perfect for what I want to talk to you about today. Shared vulnerability. That's what we're after here," says Mr. Ward.

"What is shared vulnerability?" asks Val.

"Yes," says Li. "Please explain."

"Happy to," says Mr. Ward. "The reason I have you do free writes and share some of your most private thoughts and experiences with each other is so you can learn to trust one another with your stories. I want you to see that we all have things we're sensitive about. We all have complex lives, we all have wounds, and we all have struggles."

Struggles. Yeah. That's something I know about.

"Some of the best poems, the poems that touch us most deeply, are personal stories," says Mr. Ward. "That's especially true with slam poetry. And if we're going to write and perform poetry like that in front of strangers, we need to feel strong about it. We need to feel supported. This room is your safe place, and the girls in this circle are your support group. It's important that you get to know each other, to trust each other."

Val looks around the room and nods. "We get it, Mr. Ward," she says. And she's right.

"Great!" says Mr. Ward. "Then let's get started."

We open the meeting with a free write, and the poem it leads me to is more honest than any I've ever written before.

I was worried Carrie would be bored, but she seems to like hearing us do poetry, especially the group pieces. She gets all into the rhythm and claps her little hands. Besides, the other girls think she's cute and treat her like our junior mascot, coaxing her to write poems of her own. And we're starting to rub off on her. Last week, when I picked her up from school, she showed me an eight-line riff on "roses are red" she'd scribbled in her notebook. I think I'll show it to Marcel. I'll bet he gets a kick out of it. The spelling was wonky, but the poem wasn't half bad, for a squirt. Still,

I've been wishing I could come to rehearsal without her so I'd feel free to let my feelings rip. School rules are not the problem. I can't talk about Mom's fixation on alcohol, or her penchant for being missing in action, or how hard it is for me to be a kid when I'm forced to raise one that isn't even mine. With Carrie in the room, I have to bite my tongue, and it's getting pretty bloody here lately. I'll stick with it, though. Even the little bit of truth I get to spill makes my load feel a little lighter.

School Rules

by Freddie Houston

Stage right,
the lights fade on a daily life
of tiptoeing around
my niece's feelings about the mom
who traded time with her
for time spent cozying up to crank.
The truth is too rank
for her tender little-girl ears.
And so, until she's fast asleep,
I keep bitter thoughts
under my tongue's lock and key.
Have I mentioned how it hurts me?
That neither my niece nor I
manage to have a mother
worthy of the name?
Oh, mine is present,
in an alcoholic-fog kind of way,
which is to say, hardly at all.
I'll give her what faint praise is due:
Every week, she brings home
what salary remains after
her routine rendezvous
with the local liquor mart.
She's smart that way,
puts on just enough of a show
of hardworking respectability

and motherly concern
to convince the world
that all is well behind our door.
It is not. And I want more,
like a mom who truly
carries Carrie,
carries me
so I can sometimes be
the kid I am–
do homework before stopping
to make a meal,
go to parties,
be irresponsibly late
without worry that a child waits
for me at home. Alone.
I want days, weeks, months
of not overseeing my niece's care–
has she bathed?
brushed her teeth?
combed her hair?
said her prayers before
I tucked her in?
When did that become
too much to ask?
Morning approaches.
I bite my tongue
and swallow the curses that rise
whenever I look into
Mom's vacant eyes.

Stage right,
the lights come up.
Mom's running late.
No surprise.
I wake my niece
and ready her for school.
There is breakfast to be prepared,
sack lunches to be made,
a long day ahead of pretending
not to mind playing Mommy
to my sister's child.
Even when Carrie throws
a temporary tantrum,
she deserves to know
what it's like to be loved.

DARRIAN

I look around the room, notice all the girls huddled together, hanging on Freddie's every word. There's something happening with them. They seem . . . closer. Yeah. I'm pretty sure. Or maybe it's just this poem, pulling them all in, making them think about their own moms. Freddie's poem sure makes me think about mine, about how lucky I was.

I don't think I told Mami thank you enough. I don't think I ever could. I still have time to tell Papi, though.

ANGELA

Kyle's got a lot of patience. I bet that would surprise people. He loves speed, and he's the first person to challenge someone to a race, but he's good at slowing down, too. Lately, he's slowed down enough to give me skateboard lessons. Turns out he's a really good teacher. He's got me up on a skateboard. Me! On a skateboard! You should have seen the look on Mrs. Wexler's face when I told her. Priceless.

After a few lessons with him, I've gotten pretty comfortable on my board. He just bought a new one, so he loaned me his first until I can save money to buy one of my own.

It's crazy. I thought I'd be afraid of falling or hurting myself. Instead, I was mostly afraid that I wouldn't be able to handle the board at all, that I couldn't stand on it right or find the right balance, or whip up enough nerve to even try. But I was wrong.

Kyle meets me in front of my building every morning, and we skateboard to school together. We zip down the blocks, take fast corners, and even ride the curb once or twice on the way. I'm a little slow on the lingo, but when I ride, I feel peaceful inside, and when I go especially fast, Kyle says my hair looks like a red flag in the wind. I like that.

"One day, you'll be a ripper," says Kyle. That's a really good, consistent skater. Imagine!

Last week, Kyle started digging around in my head, trying to figure out what kinds of things scare me.

The streets are pretty busy at this hour, but we skateboard side by side as much as possible. We separate whenever we need to let someone pass.

We're skateboarding home after school, and an ambulance tears down the street with its siren splitting every eardrum in the city. I step off my board for a minute to cover my ears until it passes, then keep going. Kyle comes up behind me.

"That didn't scare you?"

"What?"

"The ambulance. The siren."

"No. Why should it?"

"Sirens scare a lot of people," he says.

I just shrug.

He's quiet for a block or so. Then he batters me with more questions.

"What about gunshots?"

"What gunshots?"

"You know. Sometimes there are gunshots around here. Don't you worry about that?"

I think for a minute.

"If I hear one, and I know that's what it is, I jump. But I don't, like, think about gunshots a lot, or worry about them happening, if that's what you mean."

"That's weird. What about gangs?"

"What about them?"

"Do they scare you?"

"Well, I try to avoid them. Other than that, I don't think about them much." We reach the next corner and wait for the light to turn green.

"Okay," says Kyle while we're waiting. "Then what kinds of things do you stress about?"

Good question. I can't say "everything" because I realized I'm not stressed out about gangs and gunshots. I don't like either one, but I honestly don't think about them that much. So, what makes me anxious?

"Myself, mostly. I get anxious about what's inside of me. Or what isn't."

"Huh?"

"I stress about whether people will like me or not. I'm afraid that people won't take me seriously, or that they'll only take me seriously. I'm afraid that I'm too smart, or that I'm not smart enough, or brave enough, or pretty enough for a boy to–"

Oh, God! Why did I say that out loud?

My cheeks burn. I look at Kyle out the corner of my eye and see him smiling.

What does that mean? Why is he smiling?

The light is taking too long to turn green. I check for cars, then push off with one foot on the board, the other pushing along the ground to build up speed. I reach the other side of the street and keep going, moving faster than I ever have. Half a block away, Kyle catches up. When he gets close enough to talk, he coughs like he's trying to clear his throat.

"So what you're saying is, you're afraid that you're not enough," says Kyle.

"What?"

He says it again. "Sounds to me like you're afraid of not being enough."

I don't say anything at first. I just turn his words over in my mind. Then I feel them slide around like tiles on a Rubik's Cube. One by one, they slip into place, and suddenly, the puzzle is solved.

"Yes. Yes! That's exactly it."

"I thought so."

"Wow." I don't say anything else. I go quiet and let this new idea sink in. The word *enough* echoes inside my head, pinging back and forth, until Kyle breaks the silence.

"You know that's just plain silly," he says. "Of course you're enough. Everybody is enough. I've got a fake heart valve, and I'm still enough. Think about it." Then he and his shiny new board take off flying.

I never quite catch up. Before I know it, I'm home.

Anxiety

by Angela Marie Bailey

Anxiety would be
easier to slay
if the things I feared
were outside of me.
I could take karate lessons
to fend off muggers,
learn to repel rapists
with a swift kick
in their tender places.
But it's not fear of these
that gets my knees wobbling.
No siren blare
or nightmare of gunshots
sends me running.
It's this shivering person within
who feels too thin,
too tall,
too plain-Jane,
too not-at-all what's popular,
acceptable, respectable,
stylish enough,
smart enough,
brave enough,
lovable enough–
Enough!

It's time for me
to tell that mixed-up girl
in the mirror that,
as a matter of fact,
she's more than enough.
She's plenty.

DARRIAN

GOOD AND PLENTY—NOT JUST CANDY ANYMORE

Never heard anybody call herself *plenty* before. I like it. I may just have to borrow the word, myself.

It's crazy watching Angela grow, watching everybody in class move up to the next level.

Am I growing, too? Who gets to measure?

Maybe I'll ask Li what she thinks.

JENESIS

"What's it like, going to a foster home?"

That's what Angela asks me after our last slam rehearsal. Now that we're becoming a team, she figures it's safe to ask, and I don't mind. I shrug, then say, "The hard part is waiting for the other shoe to drop."

She cocks her head, confused, of course.

"What I mean is, from the minute you set foot in a new home, you're waiting for the social worker to tell you it's time to leave," I tell her. "You're always moving, moving, moving, going from one home to the next. And nobody ever tells you why. Maybe the people don't like you. Maybe the foster parents decide it's hard enough to look after their own kids. Maybe they treat you like a slave, and you let it slip when the social worker calls to ask you how it's going. Whatever. One day, it's time to move on. And even though you think you're ready for it, you never really are."

There's more to it, of course. The wishing you had a family of your own; the dying to belong somewhere, to someone who looks like you; the constant feeling of being all alone in the universe.

And then there's something worse: the fear that soon, you'll have no foster home to go to at all. What then?

But I'm not spilling my guts, not to Angela. Not yet. So I stick with the whole business of goodbye, knowing I'll have to say it sooner or later, but never knowing when. That's enough revelation for one afternoon.

Time to Go

by Jenesis Whyte

It always feels like an ordinary day
whenever the time comes
for me to shuffle from
one home to the next.
Some people say
home is where the heart is,
but they've never needed
a map to locate
the city or state
or the building
their belongings
should be shipped to,
not that I have that many.
Don't feel sorry for me, though.
I'm an expert at
the hasty retreat.
My feet are veterans
of the quick goodbye.
(Thirteen foster homes and counting.)
The social worker
gives me my marching orders
on the telephone.
Hey, I don't even groan.
Swapping out one
half-remembered address
for another is simply

part of my routine.
I say goodbye to the strangers
who never learned what memories
cut me in the night,
causing my tears
to run like blood.
I say goodbye to the floors
that failed to memorize
my footsteps;
I say goodbye
to the creaky old cot
no one even bothered
to tuck me into.
I say goodbye to the closet,
as hollow as I found it,
never having more than
one secondhand jean jacket
and one dingy white shirt
swinging from half-bent
wire hangers.
I clear the shelf
of clothes and books,
and bam! All done.
It only takes me a minute
to make all my
worldly goods disappear
inside the garbage bag
I brought here.
I say goodbye to the walls

I didn't have time enough
to tell my secrets to.
If these walls could talk,
it wouldn't matter.
They've got none of my stories
to give away.
So, hey! Why should I care
if it's time to say goodbye?
Is it difficult? Does it bite?
The answer to that
question is:
Yes. And no.
Why? Because
I hardly had a chance
to say hello.

DARRIAN

Wow. Jenesis is finally cutting loose. No more sweet little stories. No more code. I guess it's truth time.

I bet that's what Li was thinking when she looked over at me at the end of the poem and smiled.

The closer we come to the poetry slam at the end of the semester, the deeper everyone's poems get. All you have to do is check out Jenesis to know that's true.

GIRL LACES HER BOOTS FOR BATTLE

It's on.

MARCEL

I stand near the door of Mr. Ward's room, waiting for Freddie. As soon as I see her, I pounce.

"Hi!"

"Hi, yourself."

"So, I've been thinking," I say. "When are we going to go out?"

"Excuse me?" From the tone of her voice, I know I just came at her wrong.

"I mean, can we go out sometime?" I ask. Much better.

"Go out," says Freddie.

"Yeah."

"Go out," she repeats.

"Uh, yeah."

"You remember my niece?"

"Yeah. Carrie."

"Well, taking care of her doesn't leave a lot of time for going out."

"Oh. Right." So now I feel like an idiot. Then I get an idea.

"Then how about I come visit you."

"I'm not sure you'll want to do that," says Freddie. "My home ain't no picnic these days."

I shrug. "Mine neither."

Freddie bites her bottom lip and thinks for a minute.

"What if our visit gets interrupted? What if my mom comes home drunk and I have to help put her to bed?"

I shrug. "I'll help."

Freddie studies my face to see if I'm serious.

"Okay."

"Okay?"

"Yeah. Come over after school."

"Cool."

"Cool," says Mr. Ward, "is what's going on inside the classroom."

I jump back a little. I didn't even see him roll up.

"Good one, Mr. Ward." I wave my hand toward the door. "After you."

Out the corner of my eye, I catch Freddie grinning.

I go home in a decent mood, call Mom at her first job to let her know I'll be out for a while. I'm hunting for a soda in the fridge, so I've got her on speaker.

"Don't come home too late," she tells me. "And watch yourself out there, Marcel."

Pops chimes in. "Yeah, and if you see a cop, you run!"

Business is slow at the restaurant, so Pops is home early.

"Don't tell that boy to run!" Mom yells through the phone. "You want to get him killed?"

"It's that or go to prison," he says. "What's the difference? Either way, his life is over."

There's no arguing with Pops when he's on a rant. I

take Mom off speaker. "I'll be fine, Mom," I tell her. I can tell she's tired. Her voice is practically scraping the floor. Last thing she needs is to worry about me. "I won't be out that late. I got school tomorrow, remember."

"So long as *you* remember," Mom says, and she hangs up.

I forget about the soda and gather up my stuff to head on over to Freddie's.

An hour later, I get to see Freddie in action. One minute, she's playing with her niece, the next she's helping her with homework, the next she's doing dishes and setting the table for dinner. Meanwhile, I try working on my own homework to keep out of her way, but I can't concentrate. All I want to do is watch Freddie do her thing. I don't know how she does it all.

Oh, and her mom does come home drunk. I jump up to help, but Freddie asks me to stay with Carrie instead. Keep the little squirt company. Keep her distracted is more like it.

Once her mom's in bed, Freddie finishes cooking up some sloppy joes. Nothing special, but it was good. I do the dishes while she tucks the squirt in for the night.

She walks back into the living room and I ask, "When do you do your homework?"

"Now," says Freddie, yawning.

I shake my head. "How do you do it?"

Freddie takes her time answering. "I think about tomorrow, the life I want to build–a good life. College. Good job. Nice home for me and the squirt. Only way I can get there is to work hard, study hard. Keep looking forward."

"Don't you ever get pissed off? 'Cause this here is not fair—you taking care of a kid that's not even yours, and taking care of your mother on top of it. That's plenty without school. If I was you, I'd be mad all the time."

"You *are* mad all the time," says Freddie. "At least, you used to be. Seems like you're a little better lately."

"I guess. But you still didn't answer the question."

"I am mad, sometimes," says Freddie. "I just don't hold on to it like you do. There's no percentage in that, now, is there? Better to use my energy to hang on to hope and fight for something better."

I nod. Freddie's right. I guess I should try that.

Hope, huh? Okay. I'll give that a shot.

Freddie and I sit quietly, finish our homework together.

JENESIS

Yesterday, for some reason, Li asked if I'd taken the SATs early, or if I'm planning on taking them later. What's the point? Sure, I wish I could go to college, but wishes are like fairy dust, and there ain't no fairies in my neighborhood. Right now, college is a dream, and I'm too wide awake to have one.

Taking the SAT won't help me find a place to live once I turn eighteen. That's when the government checks stop. That's when I get kicked out on my butt. No more foster care. No more roof over my head. And guess what? No choice in the matter.

Shit. I turn seventeen this year, eighteen next year. I wouldn't mind staying seventeen for a while. In fact, forever sounds good. Yeah. I could make that work. All I need to do is find me a vampire.

Studying for the SATs? Riiiight. I need to be studying how not to look scared for when I end up living on the street. I can't tell Li that, though. She wouldn't get it. How could she? She's never had to think about how to make it on her own. She's lucky. Lots of these kids are. They gots no idea.

Tick Tock

by Jenesis Whyte

Tick tock. Tick tock.
Eighteen is the clock
my life is set to.
Tick tock. Tick tock.
On that day,
my social worker will say,
"Jenesis, it's time.
No more foster home
for you.
Get your books stacked,
get your clothes packed.
Don't dawdle. Don't stop."
So what if I've got
nowhere else to go?
The Sword of Damocles
I once read about
is scheduled to drop,
primed to chop the head
off of my tomorrow.
I refuse to entertain sorrow,
but I know enough to
forget cable-sweater dreams
of Ivy League campuses
and wild celebrations
of so-called "independence"
fueled by booze or beer at

adolescent all-nighters,
passively permitted by
proud parents because
their kiddos' next four years
will be marked by
endless hours of serious
higher educational pursuit.
But that's their story.
Tick tock. Tick tock.
On my eighteenth birthday
the clock stops,
and I'm out on my
beautiful Black butt.
But that can't be it.
I've come too far,
have hung on too long
for my whole future to fit
inside a garbage bag
labeled Your Luck
Has Run Out.
Please!
Don't tell me
my beautiful Black mind
is a terrible thing to waste
if you're gonna let the world
toss it aside.
Please!
Say there's a way out,
a way up.

Please!
Fill my cup
with enough kindness
to carry me
at least until
tomorrow.

DARRIAN

Wow. I don't think anyone in the room was breathing through that whole thing.

"Thank you, Jenesis," says Mr. Ward in a soft voice. "I hope you were all paying attention, because that, ladies and gentlemen, is what slam poetry is about."

Mr. Ward's right. She taught us all something. I know she taught me.

I figured being in foster care was tough, but I didn't know it ends when you turn eighteen.

FOSTER SYSTEM SHORT-CIRCUITS

I'm glad I got Papi. He would never kick me to the curb.

There isn't time for anyone else to read after Jenesis. When the bell rings, Mr. Ward asks her to stay.

Wonder what that's all about? I ask myself. So, being a nosy newsman, I listen.

Mr. Ward says he wants to sit down with Jenesis and have a talk. He asks if she has a few minutes to meet with him after school over the next couple of days. She shrugs, which, in Jenesis-speak, means "okay."

Maybe Mr. Ward can help her. I hope so.

I never did get around to asking her why she's not happy looking so different, so special. But she's got so much going on in her life, that hardly seems important now.

TEAM GIRLZ: **VALENTINA**

"Ladies," says Mr. Ward at the beginning of rehearsal, "I could use a little help. We need to put together a flyer to advertise the poetry slam, and we need somebody to design it. Any takers?"

Mr. Ward may be out of luck. No one is raising her hand.

"I'll help," says Li.

Guess I was wrong.

"I can do a little calligraphy," she mentions.

"Thanks, Li. Let me show you what I have in mind. Meanwhile, ladies, talk amongst yourselves," says Mr. Ward.

"No problem," says Freddie. "We need to start thinking about a group poem, anyway."

"Yeah. And choreography," says Jenesis. "We gots to have cool moves!"

"Seriously. What's our group poem going to be about?"

Angela surprises us by piping up first. "We're girls. So let's write about that. You know: how other people see us—"

"Yeah," says Freddie. "Like boys."

"Yes," says Angela. "So, how do most boys see us?" We throw the idea around.

"Like babies."

"Like weaklings."

"Right!"

"Not in my family," says Li, rejoining the group. "It's not allowed!"

"Well," says Freddie, "you're probably the exception."

"Most of them treat us like Barbies," says Angela.

"Not in my culture," I say. "Boys learn pretty quick that we are strong. But, like my papa taught me, most boys think we're only good for one thing, and we know better."

"Preach!" says Jenesis.

"We are badass women," says Freddie.

"Woman warriors," adds Li.

"You got that right! Let's do this," says Jenesis.

"But how? Mr. Ward, do you have any ideas?" asks Angela.

"Why don't each of you do a free write on the subject, then pull out some of the best lines from each, and shape your group poem from there."

"Sounds good to me," says Freddie. "What do y'all think?"

Everyone agrees, so we get busy.

Ten minutes later, we've got a place to start and Jenesis is back to talking about choreography.

"We could stand in a line, with our backs to the audience," she says, "then turn around one by one to perform our section of the poem, and flip back around and pose while the next girl goes."

"Or," says Li, "we could be in chairs, like, um–what is

that game called, where you walk around a group of chairs while music plays, and then, when the music stops, you sit in the nearest chair, and there's always one person left standing?"

"Musical chairs!" says Angela.

"Right!" says Li. "Only, in our version of the game, the last person standing steps forward to perform her poem. Then, when she's done, the music starts up again."

"Or, what about, instead of music," I say, getting into the spirit, "we all hum or chant something like, 'Tell it! Tell it! Tell it!' And we stop and take our seats just in time for the next girl to perform her poem."

"Oooh," says Jenesis. "I like the way you think."

"Or," says Freddie, with a twinkle in her eyes, "we could dance around the circle."

"You mean like this?" Jenesis rises to her feet and throws her hips from side to side, and we all crack up. Even Mr. Ward, who's supposed to be busy grading papers in the back of the room.

"Y'all laugh all you want," says Jenesis, "but you know I look good!" She keeps shimmying and shaking in a wide circle, and we laugh so hard, we can hardly breathe.

"One more thing," says Jenesis. "We need to hit the stores. I've got a few coins from babysitting, and I want to buy me something cute for the slam. Plus, we have got to take Miss Li shopping, 'cause I am not getting onstage with her looking like some lost little boy, swimming inside some boring old sweats that are two sizes too big!"

Li blushes, but she smiles a little, too.

"Okay," she whispers. Angela throws an arm around Li's waist and gives her a squeeze.

"Well, all right!" says Jenesis. "We gonna have ourselves a good old shopping time!" She and Freddie high-five each other, and the rest of us are all grins.

I suddenly realize, even though I speak two languages, I can't find a single word that says how much I love the people in this room.

JENESIS

I go straight to my room one night after slam rehearsal, and Karen turns up at my bedroom door.

"You haven't been around much lately. Not that I care."

"Aww. You miss me," I say, dripping sarcasm.

"Hardly," says Karen, but she's still taking up space in my doorway. "You've probably been getting into some kind of trouble."

"Right."

"So? What have you been up to?"

"Rehearsals," I tell her. Why not?

"Rehearsal for what?"

"A poetry slam."

"A poetry slam?"

"Is there an echo in here?"

Next thing I know, this girl is bouncing into my room, putting her skinny little butt on my bed. What?

"I went to a poetry slam once. Those things are cool!"

"You. You've been to a poetry slam."

"Uh-huh."

"Oooh-kay." Not sure I'm buying it, but–whatever. "Well, I'm happy for you. Now, can you please leave? I've got homework to do."

Karen doesn't move an inch. "Tell me about the slam first," she says, swinging her legs over the side of my bed.

"What are we, best friends all of a sudden?" The girl doesn't even blink.

"Just tell me, and I'll go away." I can see she means it.

"Fine."

I take a deep breath and tell her all about Mr. Ward's class, Open Mike Friday, and Mr. Ward's idea to do a poetry slam.

"Each team meets for rehearsals at school after hours. So, that's the story. Now go!"

Karen flinches at the sound of my voice, then finally slides off the bed and takes a step toward the door.

She turns back one last time before leaving.

"So, when is it?" she asks.

"Like I'd tell you! Get. Gone!"

What is with this girl tonight? She has never cared two licks what I do, one way or the other. Now all of a sudden she's in my face about this poetry slam. Can you imagine Miss Priss sitting through a poetry slam? The idea makes me want to laugh, but I hold it in.

"Good. Night," I tell Karen. Finally she leaves.

That's the most conversation we've had since I've been here. Weird. I wonder if that's what having a pesky sister would be like. Guess I'll never know.

Okay. Where's my notebook for English?

Equation

by Jenesis Whyte

I've been trying to solve
the mathematics of sisterhood,
not that I'm part of one,
but why should that keep me
from wondering whether
Sister + Sister = Love, or Crazy?
I can hardly tell
from the silly sitcom world
of distilled kinship dysfunction.
Didn't I read somewhere
that the happy homemaker
nuclear family
is a myth?
Love is real, though.
And friendship.
I've felt the multiplication
of their magic,
the way the love of a friend
can swell the heart.
With each home swap,
I've somehow managed
to gather a few friends
to count, and count on,
which makes me think
Friend + Friend + Me

May just be
the best family equation
of all.
At least, it's one
I get to call
Mine.

DARRIAN

Sometimes, girls make me jealous—the way they push past the stupid stuff that divides them so they can stick together when it counts. Jenesis is right, calling it a kind of magic. Too bad most of us guys can't figure out that trick.

LATEST TRENDS IN MACHO MALE BONDING

Yeah, that would make the news!

TEAM BOYZ: **KYLE**

I roll into slam rehearsal just as Mr. Ward is about to announce the free-write theme.

"The poetry slam is coming up fast, and I want you guys to really stretch yourselves. Today's free-write theme is 'metamorphosis.' Now, it may take you a few minutes to come up with a response, but that's okay. I'll give you fifteen minutes for this one," says Mr. Ward.

"Metamorphosis, huh?" says Tyrone.

"Do you need any help?" asks Mr. Ward.

"No," says Tyrone. "I got this."

"That makes one of us," I say under my breath.

"My other classes been keeping me pretty busy lately, but I haven't lost my touch, Teach."

"Glad to hear it," says Mr. Ward. "Oh! Before I forget, I wanted to let you know that I've invited a few guest poets to join us at the poetry slam. Team Boyz is a little light, even with Tyrone here, so I've asked Wesley Boone and Raul Ramirez to step in. They're also poets from last year's Open Mike series. They won't be collecting points like you, though, but they will help to fill out the program."

"Cool!" says Tyrone. "Wesley is my homeboy!"

"Okay. Back to the free write," says Mr. Ward. "Fifteen minutes."

Two minutes in and my blank page is still staring back at me.

Metamorphosis. Metamorphosis. Instead of opening up my mind, the word is shutting it down. So I think about what it means. Change. Alteration. Transformation. Ah!

Finally, I start to write.

My mother has hated my skateboard since day one. Whenever she looked at it–or me riding it–she imagined disaster. But skateboarding is fun.

Then I got this crazy idea: I'll teach my mom to skateboard! Why not? I taught Angela, and she's doing just fine.

So, one day, I offer my mom lessons. She bristles at first, but I keep after her.

"Come on, Mom. Angela took lessons, and she used to be practically afraid of her own shadow."

"I know, but–"

"Come on. Don't be a chicken."

I start making clucking sounds, and that does it.

"Okay. Okay. One lesson," she agrees.

I teach her the basic stance, show her how to push with one foot on the board, the other on the street. Once she builds up a little speed, I lead her down the block and back. I'm mostly hoping she won't bail or see the dark side of the board before it's all over. That's not exactly what happens.

She wants to do it again.

"You sure?" I ask her.

"I'm sure," she says. And you know what she sounds like? Me, when I was a little kid on Christmas, trying out a new toy.

Now my mom wants to go skateboarding. With me. On weekends!

What have I done?

Mom's even started to look up skate park locations! I tell her to take it slow. Tell her we should stick to street skating. Meanwhile, Dad is laughing his head off, but Mom doesn't care. She's into it now.

This is not the monster I was trying to create, but you know what? My mom's quit looking at my board like it's a coffin.

Boom! Metamorphosis.

I finish my free write a little ahead of time, so I just lean back in my chair and close my eyes. Pictures of my mom on a skateboard roll through my mind, and I just sit there, grinning.

Butterfly

by Kyle

You see them
flying around each summer,
delicate wings flashing
bits of rainbow color
as they flit
here, there, and everywhere.
I know. I know. We guys
tend to see butterflies
as girly, but think about
what they've been through.
They start off as wormlike
caterpillars courageously dodging
fast-footed boys
determined to shorten
their life span.
The few who make it
go through alteration,
transformation,
metamorphosis,
change, which is
the hardest thing of all.
Even the word change
is tough enough
to leave me bloody.
I don't know about you,
but I don't like to change

my shirts, my sheets, my mind
unless I'm forced to.
So what could be more macho
than a caterpillar voluntarily
entering a cocoon
with no notion of what he'll be
when he comes out?
If you ask me,
metamorphosis is
pretty badass.

DARRIAN

If you told me "badass" and "macho" were gonna come out of that skinny little gringo's mouth, I'd have called you a liar. But Kyle is full of all kinds of surprises. Good ones, though. Forget the book cover. You've got to look inside.

TRUTH PLAYS HIDE-AND-SEEK

TEAM BOYZ: **MARCEL**

We're almost ready for the poetry slam, but not quite.

"Okay, y'all," Tyrone says at our last rehearsal. "We gots to get our group poem down. You feel me?"

We all nod.

Darrian turns to Tyrone. "You got a theme in mind, *ése*?"

"Not really," says Tyrone.

I got an idea, but I want to hear what somebody else is gonna come up with. A few minutes pass, and all I hear is a lot of nothin'. I'm about to speak when Mr. Ward steps in.

"How about loss, or losing?" says Mr. Ward.

"Naw, Teach," says Tyrone. "Don't nobody want to think about losing."

"I know," says Mr. Ward, "but in reality, everyone loses something, or someone, at some point in life. It's a great universal subject. Just give it a chance, see where it takes you."

The whole time he's talking, I'm thinking, *Hell no.*

Sure, I know about loss. Lost my friends when we had to move from our old apartment after Pops went to jail, 'cause felons can't live in Section 8 housing. The only way we could've stayed was if Moms and Pops got divorced, and Moms wouldn't. Lost having Moms around as much 'cause she had to take a second job to pay for food and a new place with no help from Uncle Sam. Lost the Pops I used to know. And justice. I used to think it was something everybody was guaranteed, but that idea got knocked out of me good. Guess I should count that as a loss, too.

Yeah, I know about loss, but I sure as hell don't want to write about it. I've already done that plenty. Besides, it doesn't hurt as much as it used to, now that I've learned to let it out, to put it into poetry. Now I want to write about something else. Something better.

"Hope," I say out loud.

"What was that?" asks Mr. Ward.

"We need an idea for a group poem? Let's write about hope."

What was it that Freddie said? Use your energy to hang on to hope.

I look around at Tyrone, Kyle, Darrian, then back at Mr. Ward.

"You say we should write about loss. Well, you lose hope, what else is there?"

Mr. Ward flashes me one of his secret smiles, like I just made his day.

"I like that," he says. "Okay, gentlemen. 'Hope.' That's our new subject. You've got fifteen minutes to do your free write. Go!"

Darrian gives me a nod, and we all get down to business.

Hope

by Tyrone Bittings
Kyle Newton
Marcel Dixon
Darrian Lopez

High expectation
is not exactly a station
near the subway stop
where I live,
so let me give you
some advice:
If you hope to hope
for more than a minute,
you better be prepared
to put your whole heart in it.
First up,
you gotta believe, 'cause
desire accompanied by expectation
requires confidence,
confidentially speaking.
Hope is for the strong,
not for the weak, yo.
And I would know.
The heart can be a fragile thing,
but we forget.
It's hidden so deep
inside the chest,
the beats are imperceptible, unless

fear, anxiety, exertion
make the heart race,
thunder violently against
the rib cage,
a rage of blood bringing it
to a full stop, or skip,
leaving us in that netherworld
halfway between life and death,
the end of breath,
if only for a second.
I'm a seasoned traveler
to that distant place,
my heart a fragile passenger
riding on the will
God still gives me
to be here
one more day,
to hope for one more
tomorrow.
Confidentially speaking,
hope is for the strong,
not for the weak, yo.
And I would know.
Hope is the nightstick I swing
to bludgeon memories of a past
that would blast my future
if I let it.
Hope is the power
poetry has given me

to channel the righteous rage
that would otherwise
rip me apart.
Hope heals my hurt, my heart,
leaves me room to breathe,
gives me the mustard seed
of faith I need
to press on, to offer
something worthwhile
to my family, my girl,
the world.
Confidentially speaking,
hope is for the strong,
not for the weak, yo.
And I would know.
Ever since cancer carried
mi madre *from this world,*
hope has been the headline
of my life,
the story that's always
the news we need,
the inspirational tale
I want to tell, report, repeat
on the front page of the daily news,
or, to be more precise,
the New York Times
I plan to be on,
in the future I hope for
and help to create

every time I spin
a hot headline
for the high school paper.
Time may not heal all wounds,
but hope takes the edge off
of heartache.
Confidentially speaking,
hope is for the strong,
not for the weak, yo.
And I would know.
We stand here,
sturdy in our truth,
a band of badass youth
ready to take on tomorrow,
armed to the teeth
with holsters full of hope.
Confidentially speaking,
hope is for the strong,
not for the weak, yo.
And we? We know.

VAL

The slam is a week away, and everybody is getting a little antsy, especially the boys, who keep trash-talking about how they're going to dominate. For sure, they're going to be the loudest!

We're all excited. There are flyers posted all over the school! Lots of kids have told me they're planning on coming. I'm glad, but a little nervous, too.

I can't wait to meet Raul Ramirez. I hear he's pretty cute. Not that I'm looking for a boyfriend, but it never hurts to have a cute boy around.

Yesterday, the girls' slam practice ran a little late. We worked on our group poem, and it took forever to nail down the timing. It didn't help that I kept forgetting my lines. I've never had to memorize this much stuff before, but I can't perform the piece right if I don't get off book and know every word by heart. I'm not worried, though. That's what I keep telling myself. Maybe by tomorrow, I'll actually believe it.

I look around this classroom, study everybody in it: Tyrone, Jenesis, Freddie, Kyle, Li, Darrian, Marcel, and all the others. We live in the same city, go to the same school, but each of us has a different story. What we have in common is trying to figure out how to tell it. So why am I going crazy, shaving off pieces of myself, trying to fit in? Nobody fits in. We're all separate pieces, stitched together with words and friendship mostly, and somehow, it works. Maybe that's what being American is about–being different, standing out, but standing together.

My father's right. I don't need to change my name. I never did.

We Are

by Freddie Houston
Jenesis Whyte
Valentina Alvarez
Angela Marie Bailey
Li Cheng

Look at us.
We are all about being pretty
smart, pretty
strong, pretty
elevated, pretty
educated, pretty
motivated to tear down
whatever walls
others fabricated
to slow our gait
and keep us from reaching
our fullest potential.
It is essential
that we stay pretty
determined to turn
our will into skill,
to mold our inherent ability
into economic stability
for the future.
We are pretty
certain that the curtain of success
will rise on our tomorrow

if we simply borrow
and build upon the strength
of a powerful panorama of pretty
remarkable women who
came before:
women who traveled to space,
took their place on the Senate floor,
swore oaths to serve the Supreme Court,
counted themselves among the best
entrepreneurs, educators, entertainers,
poets, pilots,
designers, dancers,
emcees, MDs,
firefighters, financial wizards,
wing-walkers,
psychologists, psychiatrists,
psych-you-out spies
for, say, the Civil War Union Army.
Look at us.
Are we capable
of being more than
sassy swiveling hips and
red-painted pouting lips and
whatever cup size
you have in mind?
Give us a minute
and you'll find
we women are pretty–amazing.

LI

The slam is finally here. Tonight.

I stand in front of the bathroom mirror for a minute and take a deep breath.

"Here goes."

I dab a little blush on each cheek, then turn my head from left to right.

"Not bad."

Then I pull out the tube of lip gloss Valentina helped me pick out. I study my naked lips, then cover them with a few swipes of color.

"Almost done."

I pull the rubber band from my ponytail and let my hair fall loose. I comb it to one side and hold it in place with a silver comb I borrowed from my mother. Finally, I step back to get the full effect.

"Oh!"

Something spills down my cheek and I don't wipe it away. I just keep staring at my reflection. The girl in the mirror is almost–pretty.

MaMa was wrong. You can be pretty, and have a boyfriend, and still be smart, all at the same time. You don't always have to choose.

The phone rings, and I break away from the mirror and finish dressing. I put on a new pair of tight jeans and a bright red shirt with matching wide belt that shows off my waist.

I gather my notebook, even though I've memorized my poems, and I go downstairs.

"Ooh!" says BaBa when he sees me.

"Daughter!" says my mother. "Fancy."

"Well," I say, "tonight is special. All the kids are dressing up." Then I add, casually, "Many of their parents will be coming." I say this without looking either of them in the eye. I don't want them to feel judged for not coming to hear me read.

"I don't understand why you have to go do this–this reading," says my father.

"I told you before, BaBa. I'm going because I want to, not because I have to."

My mother grunts.

I ignore her, clutch my notebook, grab my small purse, and finally look her in the eye.

"I know poetry is not important to you, but it is important to me," I tell her. "MaMa, you know, growing up, I always wanted to learn Mandarin. All of my friends got to go to Chinese school and learn the language of their parents, but not me. You wouldn't send me or my brother because you wanted us to just be American and only speak English.

"Every day, I hear you and BaBa speaking Mandarin and I can pick up a word of two, but not much, and that makes me sad. Well, MaMa, I may not have learned Mandarin, but I did learn a special language of my own: poetry. I'm sorry you can't speak it, but I have friends who do, and I need to be with them tonight. I'm sorry if that displeases you.

"I promise to return home as soon as the slam—as soon as the poetry reading is over."

Then I walk out the door before I lose my nerve. It isn't every day I talk back to my parents!

DARRIAN

Mr. Winston, the librarian, was right. Studying poetry has taught me new ways to use language. Better yet, taking this class meant I got to meet some of the most newsworthy kids around, not to mention finding a girlfriend. Plus, I get to do a poetry slam for the first time. I've got so much material for a feature article, it was easy talking the editor of the yearbook into give me the space to write one.

JUNIOR NEWSMAN NABS HEADLINE

Now all I need to finish off the story is the name of the poetry slam's winning team.

I can hardly believe it's almost over already. In one way, it seems like we've been practicing our poems forever. In another way, it feels like we just got started. Crazy.

The last few weeks, even Papi started getting anxious, asking over and over again, "When is your poetry festival?"

"Poetry *slam*, Papi," I corrected him. "It's in a few weeks."

Now, at last, the big day is here.

The auditorium is jam-packed. Kyle's folks are here, and Angela's.

I notice a little girl who looks like she could be Freddie's sister, then I realize it must be Freddie's niece, Carrie. She's sitting with Angela's family.

Jenesis doesn't have any family in the audience, not unless you count that girl nodding in her direction.

"Well, I'll be damned," says Jenesis.

"What?" I ask.

"It's Karen. From my foster home. She said she was coming, but I didn't believe her."

"Why'd you invite her, then?"

"I didn't," snaps Jenesis.

"Hey! Don't bite my head off, *chica*!"

"Sorry."

There's one other person here for Jenesis, some woman sitting next to Mr. Ward's wife. Jenesis stares at the lady for a long time. Later, I find out it's a lady from Inspire Life Skills Training, an organization that helps foster kids after they turn eighteen and have to leave the system. From what Jenesis tells us, she's going to need help like that.

The lady is there to talk to Jenesis about a new beginning. You can tell it's a good thing, because Jenesis looks like someone switched on a light behind her eyes.

Valentina's family takes up half a row. Exactly how many relatives does that girl have, anyway?

Then I see Li. At least, I think it's Li. Her hair is loose, falling over her shoulders. She's got on a bright red top that fits her just right, and her lips are darker than usual. Is she wearing lipstick? Whatever. Li looks—wow.

I don't see Li's parents with her, but she said they probably wouldn't come. I can't wait for a chance to steal a kiss. It will be easier without her parents around. Still, too bad they're not here to check out what an amazing poet she is.

I keep looking around, checking off parents and trying to find Papi. I have a hard time picking him out, but I know he'll be here. I finally spot him a few rows back. The second I see him, I wave like a little kid. So much for trying to look cool!

And guess who's sitting right behind Papi? Zeke and Shorty from the neighborhood! Shorty's eyes catch mine and he gives me a thumbs-up. And I haven't even done anything yet.

ANGELA

For once, I'm not the only one ready to jump out of her skin. Everybody backstage is pacing, half wishing the curtain would go up already, half wishing it wouldn't. Except for Val and Tyrone. Tyrone and his buddy Wesley are deep in conversation. Catching up, I guess. As for Val, she's too busy eyeing Raul Ramirez to be nervous. Can't blame her, though. He's as cute as everyone said.

I peek out into the audience and notice a few people holding paddles. One says 1, another says 2, and one says 2.5. They're judging paddles, and the numbers go up to 5.

Tyrone says in most slams there are twenty-five poets, so you only get to present two poems each. There are fewer of us, though, so there will be three rounds, and each of us will get to present three poems, plus our group poems. You have to perform them, though, not read them, which means we've all been cramming like crazy to memorize every word. Whenever I stumble over a line, I think, *Thanks, Mrs. Wexler!* Then I begin the poem over again.

Speaking of Mrs. Wexler, that's her sitting in the front row, right next to my mother! Guess she wants to check on her special project, meaning me. I'm glad she came, though. I wouldn't be here if it weren't for her. Joining

Mr. Ward's class turned out to be a good thing, after all. I'll say hello to her later. I might even admit that she was right. Or not.

I wish there weren't any judges for this thing. After each poem, the judges will raise their point paddles and someone–Mr. Ward, I think–will write down the scores. I don't even want to know mine. I just want to do my poems. That's it. I'm kind of looking forward to the group poem, though. I know it's worth five points, easy.

I take a deep breath, close my eyes, and repeat: "It's going to be fine. It's going to be fine." Why? Because I am enough. I. Am. Enough.

Little by little, my heartbeat slows to an easy rhythm. I am calm. I feel confident. Kyle is right. I *am* plenty, and now I'm finally beginning to believe it.

I hear the curtain rising. I open my eyes and step into place beside my team. It's showtime.

"Good evening, everyone," says Mr. Ward. "Welcome to our first poetry slam!"

DARRIAN

Boom! *Así como así,* the slam is over, and we're waiting for the final score. It's impossible to tell which team is ahead. Most of us were too busy trying to remember our lines to keep up with the count. I figure it's close, though. Still, I have my fingers crossed.

Mr. Ward studies the score sheet for the longest. He looks from one team to the other, then out at the audience. When he finally speaks, he says the one thing nobody expects.

"Ladies and gentlemen, we'll call this a draw," says Mr. Ward.

A chorus of "What?" goes up around the auditorium. At first, people onstage are grumbling, too, especially the boys. But then Tyrone, whose poems were as good as anybody's, steps forward and grabs the mike.

"Guys, we best take what we can get, because honest to God, we all know Team Girlz killed it."

A big whoop shoots up from all the girls in the audience. A few boys still grumble, but most of us have to nod our heads. That's when I turn to the girls' team and start clapping. One by one, every other guy on the team joins me. Applause spreads like a wave until the entire audience is on its feet, clapping, cheering, and whistling for Team Girlz. If you ask me, it's a beautiful thing.

The girls lift their arms in triumph, then hurry off the stage. Tyrone gives Jenesis a high five, and I bow to Li and Valentina. I'm surprised that Angela doesn't look like a deer in headlights. She actually managed to get through the whole slam without fainting or choking on her words, which was something for her. "You did it!" Kyle tells her. Angela starts smiling like her face had invented it.

Mr. Ward is smiling, too.

"So what'd you think, Mr. Ward?" I ask him, taking out my notebook and pen. A good newsman gets all the quotes he can, right?

"I think we should do this again next year," he says. "Are you up for that, Darrian?"

I think about the best way to answer his question. I think about why I came to his class in the first place. And then I look up at him and say, "Once you teach a bird to fly, you should expect him to use his wings."

Mr. Ward grabs my shoulder and gives it a warm squeeze.

"I'll see you, Darrian," he says.

"See you, Mr. Ward."

I reach for Li's hand, and we leave the auditorium together. Just as we get to the exit, I notice an old Chinese couple slipping out. I think it's Li's parents.

"Li, look!" I point to Mr. and Mrs. Cheng. I've never seen my girl's face light up like that. She looks from them, to me, and back again. I'm supposed to introduce her to

Papi, and then we were going to hang out for a while with the rest of the gang and celebrate, but . . . I give her a kiss on the cheek and whisper, “Go. I’ll catch up with you tomorrow.”

Li’s hand slips from mine, and she runs to catch up with her parents. I’m happy they came. That’s plenty for her to celebrate.

Papi is waiting for me out in the lobby. He has tears in his eyes when he sees me. My eyes are a little wet, too.

It’s been some kind of night.

Tomorrow, I’ll sit down and write that article about the slam for the yearbook. But this last headline is just for me.

BOY FINDS POETRY IN A FATHER’S TEARS

Now, that’s what you call good news.

AUTHOR'S NOTE

I hope you enjoyed *Between the Lines.* As in *Bronx Masquerade*, this novel explores the lives of many different characters. Right now, I want to focus on just one of them: Jenesis Whyte.

I spent several years in the foster care system when I was young, and as a result, I am especially sensitive to the incredible challenges experienced by teens who age out of the foster care system after their eighteenth birthday.

I was fortunate. I didn't end up on the streets, like so many former foster kids do, but I did sleep on a lot of floors, and my older sister slept on her fair share of park benches. Lots of former foster kids experience much worse, and since *Between the Lines* is a novel about teens, I wanted to take the opportunity to shine a light on this subject. I did so through the story of Jenesis Whyte, the character in foster care who will soon age out of the system. There are teens like her on nearly every high school campus across the country.

Like most teens in foster care, Jenesis faced the very real possibility of becoming homeless once her foster care status was terminated at age eighteen. As a consequence, she was at risk of becoming vulnerable to the dangers of human trafficking and the ravages of the sex trade.

The statistics for former foster kids are alarming: 50 to 70 percent of former foster youth become homeless; 25 percent of the young men end up incarcerated; and the young women are six times more likely to have babies before the age of twenty-one. In other words, the odds are very much stacked against these teens. If they are to beat those odds, they need help.

Inspire Life Skills Training, Inc., is one of the organizations that offer critical assistance to former foster youth in need. That's why I mentioned them, briefly, at the end of the novel, as a ray of hope for the Jenesis Whyte character. Jenesis may be a work of fiction, but thankfully, Inspire is not.

With six single-family homes scattered throughout Southern California's Inland Empire, Inspire's services include:

Providing affordable housing
Full-time education/job training
Life skills training
Part-time employment
Mentoring
Access to professional counseling and medical care

Those who successfully complete the program go on to attend and graduate from college or vocational school, enter the job market, and establish their own financial independence. All it takes is a deep desire, hard work, and a little help from some friends.

Inspire Life Skills Training, Inc., is based in Southern California, but there are other organizations across the nation focused on meeting the needs of former foster youth.

Are you a teen about to age out of the foster care system? If so, consider reaching out to one of these organizations for help. Offering you help is the reason they exist.

inspirelifeskills.org
covenanthouse.org
theteenproject.com
alternativesforgirls.org
agingoutinstitute.org
childrenscabinet.org
beaconinterfaith.org
communityyouthservices.org
y2yharvardsquare.org
fosterclub.com

These are just a few of the organizations waiting to give you a hand up. For additional links, check my website: nikkigrimes.com.

Asking for help to transition can be difficult, I know. But if you get that help, you'll be doing us all a favor, because, frankly, the world needs the gifts you have to offer.

Stay strong.

ACKNOWLEDGMENTS

A great deal has been said about the solitary nature of writing, and I can't argue the truth of it. However, it is also true that the journey of creating a book is one that, ultimately, draws a community of people together. Acknowledgments must be given.

Thanks to Lea Lyon, Steve and Jill Elliott, Jane Yolen, Kathy Montague, Elliot Asp, and Amy Malskeit, who generously shared work space, warm meals, listening ears, and comradeship during several all-important writing retreats at which much of this text unfolded.

Thanks to Colin North and Jennifer Larratt-Smith, who shared memories with me that helped to enrich this text.

Thanks to Dalene Parker for reading and critiquing an early draft of this work. The gift of your time is precious.

Thanks to Julie Weatherford for introducing me to and leading lively book discussions of *The New Jim Crow: Mass Incarceration in the Age of Colorblindness* by Michelle Alexander. The study of this book and the necessarily difficult conversations that followed lit a fire under me. Here, that fire led to the creation of Marcel Dixon and the story of how the War on Drugs impacted him and the life of his family.

Thanks to Kristi Perez of Inspire Life Skills and Rhonda Sciortino for guiding me to resources for foster teens who age out of the system.

Thanks, always, to my agent and friend, Elizabeth Harding, and to Montage, my arts group, for unwavering support and valuable feedback.

Thanks, finally, to the hundreds of thousands of readers of *Bronx Masquerade* who embraced the stories that issued from Mr. Ward's class, and who encouraged me to revisit that classroom for this new round of characters and stories.

Enjoy!